MW01135549

UNBREAKABLE BOND

BOOK 1 IN THE FATED MATES DUET

JESS BRYANT

- XOXO -
♡Jess Bryant

BLUE LEMON PRESS

Bless Brian

- xoxo -

UNBREAKABLE BOND

Book 1 in the Fated Mates Duet

By

Jess Bryant

Unbreakable Bond
Sometimes fate gets it all wrong.

Zoey Kent has lived with that fact ever since she turned eighteen and learned that the man she loved could never be hers. He's a born shifter, a wolf, and she's a mere human. Fate doesn't care if on paper they're a perfect pair. She isn't his fated mate and she's resigned herself to the knowledge that someday, she'll have to watch Michael mate with another. It's never crossed her mind that there might be someone else out there for her, that she would be the one to mate another, to choose another over everything she's ever known or wanted.

Sometimes fate gets it all right.

Rafe Hudson left his pack behind years ago. Physically and mentally scarred from an attack that left his parents and twin dead, he walked away from his responsibilities as Alpha. He never intended to return but lone wolf or not, he can't leave Michael open to an attack he's learned is coming for his only brother. What he didn't know was that going home would mean scenting his mate, the one person in the world that could make him whole again, that could give him everything he thought he'd lost. His pack, his home and his family.

But fate always has a plan.

There's no way Michael's brother is her future, is there? Just like there's no way that the girl his brother has loved since they were kids, was always meant to be his, right?

Only fate knows why they were brought together but there is one thing for sure, the sparks between Zoey and Rafe are undeniable. The bond between them is unbreakable. And together... they'll change the face of the pack forever.

UNBREAKABLE BOND – BOOK 1 IN THE FATED
MATES DUET

For anyone that believes in love at first sight,
or at least wants to.

CHAPTER 1

Every single woman at the party was staring at him. Hell, even the women that were already mated were staring at him. It was impossible not to. He was six plus feet of testosterone addled alpha male with rippling muscles and all of the cocky arrogance that came with that. He oozed sex, charm and power. Every female wanted to be the one that he wanted, desired above all others and claimed for eternity and they were all devastated that they weren't his mate.

Zoey Kent more than any.

He wasn't just Alpha of the pack to her. He wasn't just their leader. He wasn't just smart and sexy. He wasn't just the kindest, most loyal and caring man she'd ever known. He was all of those things but he was also so much more than that.

Michael Hudson was her best friend.

He was the man that had been there for every good day and also every bad for as long as she could remember. He was the man that took care of her and looked out for her and always had her back. He was the man that she compared all others to and he was the reason they all came up short.

He'd been her first kiss when she was fifteen. He'd been her first French kiss when she was sixteen. He'd been her first attempt at fooling around when she was seventeen. And at eighteen, if he'd scented her as his mate, she would have let him become her first and only lover.

But he hadn't.

As a natural born shifter, Michael would be mated to one female. One woman that he would want, care for and desire above all others. He would sense his female the first time they encountered each other after coming of age. An innate physiology, a mixture of scent and a recognition between two souls that was impossible to explain without the addition of a little bit of magic.

The first time it had been described to her, Zoey had swooned at the very idea. Mates. It was impossibly romantic. Plenty of people believed there was that one special person out there for them, a soulmate, but for a shifter it wasn't just a daydream but a lifelong mission to find their other half.

It was real. One person they connected with on every level. One person that understood them in every way. It was a connection that transcended simple attraction or even chemistry. It wasn't a choice based on similar hobbies or likes and dislikes, wasn't something as simple as repeating some vows that could be taken back when they didn't fit or ring true anymore.

She'd been absolutely certain that was what she and Michael had. So certain that she'd offered him her virginity before her eighteenth birthday. He was too good a guy to have accepted. Instead he'd told her that a few months was nothing to wait and do it right, to perform the ceremony and be joined forever.

They'd both been so certain that it was only a matter of time until fate proved what they already knew. That they were perfect for each other. That they were mates.

Then her eighteenth birthday had rolled around and she'd showered and dressed and readied herself for him. She'd known he would sense her break into womanhood immediately because their scents were already so linked from years spent side by side. But hours had passed as she waited for him, as she went through the motions of celebrating the day, all the while wondering where he was, and finally, when the day passed and then another and another with no contact from him, not even a word, she'd realized all of her worst fears had come true.

By the time he eventually came trudging up her driveway, head hung and shoulders hunched, despair in every step; she'd already figured it out. She might not be a wolf. She might not be a shifter. But she'd been raised here, among them, and she knew how things worked.

She and Michael weren't fated, could never be mated, and so, despite the fact that they'd loved one another for years, they couldn't be together.

It would be cheating for Michael to be with her. He hadn't met his fated mate yet. He didn't know who she was or even where she was. He didn't know when he would meet her or even if he ever would. But he'd said it would feel like cheating to be with her knowing someone else out there was meant to be his.

She'd agreed. What else was she supposed to do? Beg him to choose her over a woman that was merely a figment of his imagination at this point? Pray that even if that woman did one day show up, that he would be able to ignore his very nature and send her away? Of course not.

So she'd done the only thing she could. She'd clung to her pride. She'd ignored the hurt and the loneliness. She'd sworn that she was okay being just friends and most days, that didn't feel like a lie.

For four years, she'd controlled her feelings, her emotions and her every action when it came to her best friend. She thought she'd learned to accept what she had no control over. She thought at the very least, if she couldn't make her feelings for him go away, that she could hide them deep down where they would never again see the light of day.

On good days, she could paste on a smile and ignore the traitorous thump of her heart whenever he was in the same room. But then, on days like today when she had to watch him turn his charm and smile on every new female that came sniffing around hoping to be the woman the Pack Alpha mated, she felt like the liar she really was.

She felt human. Plain and boring and... normal. Worse, whenever she felt like this, she was reminded of just how impossible it would have been for Michael to be fated to a woman like her in the first place.

She wasn't like him. She wasn't a shifter. She wasn't a wolf. She definitely wasn't royalty like he was amongst the pack. She was nothing more than a regular girl that had been thrust into the supernatural world when she found out her adoptive parents were werewolves. She was a rarity sure, a human allowed into the inner circle, but the truth was she would always be an outsider.

There were other humans in Noir, Louisiana. Humans that had been wards or protectors of the pack for generations. Humans that had been mated with wolves and become part of the pack through that bond, bringing family in with them. There were even a handful of others like her, human children that had been taken in by pack elders through adoption at an early age.

Her mother had suffered a car accident when she was young. Even mated, she couldn't conceive. So they'd adopted Zoey. They'd given her a family. They'd given her a home. They'd given her love and support and everything that a young girl could want or need.

And somehow, without Michael, it didn't feel like enough.

God, she was a brat for even thinking that. Her parents had given her a life she'd never have dreamed of when she was in the foster system being bounced from house to house, losing touch with her biological siblings because they were separated. Her entire world had been pain and darkness back then and they'd taken her away from that. They'd brought her into this amazing world with supernatural creatures that were beautiful and deadly, savage and graceful.

She wasn't walking away, giving up her life here, just because the thought of Michael finding his mate and being forced to watch them live out their happily ever after made her physically ill.

She'd made friends here, good friends, and she'd built her business here. She'd built her life here. She could find someone here, someday, maybe, that she could love the way she loved Michael. Maybe even more. She was human so she had options, choices that the shifters around her didn't.

She could ask out a nice, normal man, get to know him and then decide if she wanted forever. Her future wasn't based on some whim of fate. So Michael wasn't hers, that didn't mean she would end up alone. There were other men in Noir, plenty of them that would be a suitable second choice for her heart.

She'd find someone else. That was life and she'd just have to get used to it. Just like she'd gotten used to the idea that Michael would never want her as more than a friend. Which was to say, she'd stomp the idea into her hard head right around the same time they started ice-skating in hell.

Downing a large gulp of her drink, she winced. She hated the taste of beer. It was what the wolves preferred so it was always served at these parties but no matter how often she tried it, she'd never come around to the taste. Even still, she took another swig from the bottle, finishing it off, before tearing her gaze away from Michael and the willowy blonde that had caught him the moment he came through the door.

He'd been late to his own party. It wasn't like him and Zoey had been worried. Even more so when he'd come storming into the room, looking around as if he was searching for someone. His eyes had landed on her and she'd thought something was wrong, that the relief coming off of him had been because he found her, but then the blonde had sauntered up to his side, his gaze had left Zoey and hadn't returned since.

She was sick and tired of reading more in his expressions, actions and words than he meant. It had to stop. She had to stop this madness once and for all. She just didn't know how to do it without breaking her own heart.

Maybe it was already broken and she'd just been fooling herself every day since she turned eighteen.

With a sigh, Zoey headed for the nearest doorway and slipped through it. She needed some fresh air. Some space and time to think. Besides, she was certain nobody would even notice she was gone.

CHAPTER 2

The pack lodge Michael had inherited from his parents was deep in the woods and backed to the river. A heavy, muggy night warmed Zoey's skin even as a cool breeze played with her dress. She slipped off her heels and left them at the edge of the porch, tiptoeing barefoot across the damp grass. She followed the path she'd been taking since childhood, easily maneuvering her way over the uneven ground until she came face to face with the tree she hadn't even realized she was looking for.

It was a cloudless night and the moon was bright. Bright enough that she could easily see the carving in the trunk of the tree. Michael's initials, a plus sign then her initials followed by the simple promise of forever. She raised her hand, tracing the carving that they'd made when she was fourteen, eight years ago, but it felt more like eighty tonight.

She couldn't explain her sudden melancholy. She'd known for years that she and Michael were done. Since the day she'd turned eighteen and he hadn't come for her, she'd known that they would never live out the fantasy life her teenage girl dreams had concocted. She'd been dealing with it for years but something was different tonight. She just couldn't put her finger on what it was.

There was a feeling in the air, something electric and powerful. She'd felt it before, on the day she found out what her parents were, on the day they'd moved here to Noir, on the day she'd become an adult. They were all important days in her life, days where she'd learned something big and essential that had changed her life forever. Then, this morning, while she was going about her business, baking at her shop she'd felt it again. Like a jolt it had hit her square in the chest... the question was, why?

Nothing out of the ordinary had happened today. Nothing made today special. Sure, Michael was hosting a party to welcome new pack members but that wasn't unusual. They'd been getting a lot of new members lately and the pack loved any reason to party, particularly before the full moon.

The full moon... She glanced up at the big orb in the sky. It wasn't tonight. If it was, she'd be locked in her house all alone as per usual and all the guests would be wearing fur and running the woods instead. She was human so the moon cycles didn't affect her and yet, she couldn't shake the feeling that this one would be different.

"Sneaking away already?"

Zoey whirled around at the sound of the voice, her heart thumping wildly in her chest. She barely contained a shriek of surprise. He'd snuck up on her, one of his many talents, and he was grinning that slightly sheepish grin that was equal parts adorable and charming.

She shrugged as she tried to calm her racing heart, "Didn't think anyone would notice."

"I did."

"You always do."

Michael smiled and she hated the small shred of wonder she couldn't keep out of her voice. The smallest crumb of attention and here she was, eating it up. Still, it was nice to know that though his attention had been on another woman as they drank and danced their way through introductions and then innuendos that he'd kept one eye on her.

He always did, but not for the reasons she wished. He'd explained it to her, more than once. If they'd simply been friends, it might have been easier, but Michael's wolf was involved, as much a part of their intense connection as their history. The bond his wolf had to her was something he understood even less than she did but he'd tried to tell her what it felt like for him.

He'd said that he loved her... but he wasn't *in* love with her.

He wasn't mated to her but his wolf cared about her, deeply, and was determined to take care of her. He'd said it was almost a feeling as if she were a member of his family. He'd said it was as if she were a beloved sister.

The brother-sister comment had felt like taking a lead pipe to the head. Her feelings for him were in no way sisterly. His certainly hadn't been brotherly before she turned eighteen when he'd stuck his tongue down her throat and copped a feel every chance she gave him.

But she supposed a teenage boy didn't have to be *in love* to want to do those things to a girl. Any girl. Particularly when said teenage boy was a shifter with enhanced alpha tendencies and raging testosterone.

"Earth to Zoey?"

"Sorry, what?" She snapped back to reality when he said her name.

"I asked if you left because you weren't having any fun or if something else drew you away."

"Oh..." She blinked, looking out over the water instead of directly at him, "I wasn't bailing. I know tonight is important to you. I just needed to get some fresh air."

"Tonight is important." He nodded, "The Gilles family will make a good addition to the pack. The parents were elders in the Crescent pack and their daughters are all young and unmated. It made the men happy to hear there would be fresh meat and several of their friends joined them for the party as well. If we're lucky, there will be mate bonds made before the night is out."

The air in her lungs tightened as he spoke and Zoey realized she wasn't breathing by the time he finished. Her mind had finally caught up with what her subconscious had been trying to tell her all day. The gut feeling that something important was going to happen, it had been trying to tell her this exact thing.

Michael was going to find his mate tonight.

She felt lightheaded. Sick. Nauseous. How had she not put it together before? It made sense. So many new faces running around town the last few days. The Gilles moving here was just the tip of it. There had been contractors working on their house, movers, even party planners all from out of town coming and going. Any one of them could be the lucky woman that would trigger Michael's wolf to recognize his mate.

Had he already seen her? Did he know who she was? Was it the blonde from inside? Was that why he'd followed her out here? To tell her that he'd found his mate?

He was still talking, "It's not only the addition of the Gilles family to the pack that we're celebrating tonight though. I haven't told anyone else but we're welcoming back a member that has been gone for a long time too, someone I didn't think was ever coming home again."

She struggled to pay attention as her mind whirled with possibilities, "You didn't mention that."

"I wasn't certain it was really happening until today." Michael scratched his jaw and sighed heavily.

"Is it a good thing or a bad thing that this person is coming back into the pack?"

Bad thing for her? Good thing for him? Was that what he was getting at?

"When he said he was coming home, that he wanted to talk, I thought it was the best news I'd ever heard, but then he got here and..." Michael trailed off, staring out across the water, lost in his thoughts and she frowned.

He? Not she? Zoey felt a small bit of relief at that but it quickly faded when she realized how stricken her best friend looked. Just as he had looked when he came rushing into the party earlier. Half-worried and half-scared, which were both foreign enough on Michael's face to worry her.

"Hey, are you okay?"

He turned to face her then and she realized how close they were standing. A deep breath would have her breasts brushing his chest. She had to crane her neck to look up at him from this angle. She wasn't short but he was far too tall for them to stand together like this comfortably. Strange that she'd never noticed their height difference until just that moment.

"You ever wish our lives weren't so complicated? No pack. No rules. Wish we could just do whatever it was we wanted, take what we wanted and not have to worry about the consequences?" He snorted, "I wasn't even supposed to be Alpha, not of the Moirae pack, and maybe that's what changed everything, changed fate."

She blinked, trying to place the look in his eyes. She didn't recognize it. She'd never seen him look at her like this before, talk to her with this edge of desperation in his tone. She had the sudden uneasy feeling that she was missing something important, that he hadn't told her something important, and the hair on the back of her neck stood up.

"Michael? What's going on?"

He reached out and gently stroked her jaw, "I wish things were different. For so long, I've known it was you, that you were the key to all of it. I thought if I could just figure out what my connection to you meant that I'd be able to fix this thing between us, because fate messed up not putting us together. You know that right?"

She leaned into his touch. She wanted to sink into him. She wanted to grab him and never let go. This moment, this was the one that she'd been waiting on for what felt like a lifetime.

Michael touching her again, touching her with all of the powerful emotion that she'd always known was there between them. Michael telling her that he wished things were different and that they could be together. But even as she stepped closer, watched his eyes stroke over her face, and even as she licked her lips, certain he was going to kiss her, she felt like she was missing something. Something important. Something about his words was off.

It was almost as if he was telling her goodbye. He was memorizing her face as if he'd never see it again. He was going to kiss her, one last time, but then what?

"Yeah, I know."

His thumb stroked softly over her cheek and his voice was low and pained when he spoke again, "I figured it out, but it wasn't what we thought."

Her mind and her body went to war. Her mouth

wanted to open, wanted to ask one of the dozen questions racing through it. Figured what out? What was it? What was he talking about? Her body wanted to shut her brain down and just accept whatever this strange moment was. Whether it was hello or goodbye or something else entirely, she didn't care.

She wanted it to last forever because she was certain the moment on the other side of this one was going to change everything.

"Michael?"

"I'm going to find a way to fix it Zo. You have to trust me. I'm going to fix it."

She didn't understand what he was talking about. She nodded anyway. It didn't matter what the question was. She trusted Michael. She always had. She opened her mouth to tell him that but she never got a word out because a loud growl stopped her short.

"Mine!"

The roar of the male voice was vicious and close enough to rattle her eardrums. She jumped. Michael's hand fell away. He winced, almost as if he was in pain, and an apologetic look crossed his face. Then, before she could even blink, he was gone.

She screamed as something huge collided with Michael and took him to the ground. Zoey staggered back, more out of shock than fear, because as she watched her brain finally caught up to what was happening. It wasn't a thing that had come flying out of the darkness to attack Michael, it was a *who*.

CHAPTER 3

Fists were flying. There was growling and snarling. Zoey felt the shimmer of magic in the air, knew that Michael was close to shifting and her gaze automatically darted to the idiot dumb enough to attack a Pack Alpha.

Her eyes widened when the attacker easily rolled Michael to his back and landed a brutal punch to the jaw that snapped his head around. Not possible, her brain screamed. He'd gotten the best of Michael and that shouldn't have been possible.

Michael was big. He was a dominant shifter. All of the male shifters she'd come across were big and muscular but Michael, being Pack Alpha, was the biggest she'd ever seen. Until now. Because she was certain from the growls, from his sheer, massive size and from the fact that he had just overpowered Michael, that the attacker was a shifter as well, possibly even another Alpha.

Because he was kicking Michael's ass.

She watched in horror as the two men, two werewolves,

rolled again, splashing into the soggy, swampy riverbed. Michael came out on top momentarily, getting what looked like a lethal hold around the other man's neck, but by the time she'd blinked he was on his back again, taking a punch to the gut this time.

Oh God, she winced at the brutal, bloody scene. What was she supposed to do? She couldn't very well get between them. She was human. They'd rip her to shreds with one misplaced swing.

"Help!" She screamed instead, "Somebody help! I need help out here!"

"Zoey." Michael choked out amid pants, "Run."

"Mine!" The attacker only growled again and slammed a fist into Michael's jaw.

"Stop it!" She screamed in horror when she heard what sounded like bones cracking, "Stop it! You're hurting him! Stop!"

Nobody was more shocked than she was when the attacker instantly stilled. It was almost as if her words had broken through his rage and he heard her. His head snapped up, his gaze connecting with hers, and she sucked in a startled breath as a flash of recognition struck her.

"Mine!"

"Goddammit, Rafe!" Michael shouted, scrambling to his feet, water splashing as he struggled back up onto dry land, "You stay the hell away from her!"

Rafe? She took a step forward, towards the two men, then caught herself and locked her legs. What was she doing? What was going on? Had he just called the other man Rafe?

"What's going on out here?"

A third male voice cut into her thoughts and she turned

in time to see Sherriff Wiley go storming past her to position himself between Michael and the other man, who had frozen on the edge of the river as soon as she spoke. She realized as they all glared at each other that Michael had put himself in front of her, blocking her from the man that had attacked him. Even still, she could feel the other man's eyes on her and her own gaze was immediately drawn back to him, past Michael, past the Sherriff, as if the only person that mattered was the one being carefully sequestered away from her.

"He's not taking her." Michael was beginning to catch his breath and his words came out steady, "This is my pack. She's part of it. He's not taking her."

"Mine!" The other man snarled and took a step forward, clearly intent on causing Michael more damage before the Sherriff shoved him the other direction.

"Get yourself under control Rafe!" Wiley ordered loudly and then lowered his voice, "I can arrest you and you can cool off in a cell at the station or you can snap to and tell me why the hell you just attacked our Pack Alpha."

"Mine!"

Almost in slow motion, Zoey watched Wiley turn to face her. His eyes were wide as he looked her over. A shiver ran down her spine when his brows furrowed and a wary, worried expression took the place of the usually staid, Sherriff's face. He glanced from her to the other man and then finally to Michael.

"Is it true?"

Michael shook his head, "No. He's unstable. You know that."

Wiley put his hands on his hips, "What I know is that he just attacked you, a Pack Alpha, something no wolf in his right mind would ever do unprovoked."

"I just told you he's out of his mind! He's practically feral!"

"Yeah, but I also know he's saying he has a claim on that girl behind you and from the looks of it, you interrupted." Wiley scowled, "You know better Michael. Nobody is allowed to interfere when it comes to a bond. Not even you."

Zoey watched the two men argue, or rather, she listened. Her eyes never left the man staring at her. He looked wild, savage and unkempt, though she wasn't sure how much of that could be owed to the violent fight he'd just won. And it was clear to her that he had won, or that he would have if he hadn't stopped when she begged him to.

His hair was unruly, falling over her his eyes in disheveled strands, and with only the moon as her light, she couldn't tell if it was black or just a really dark brown. His eyes were similarly dark, though for a second there they'd glowed with the gold of his wolf. His face was hard with its strong jaw and stubbled chin, his lips pulled tight over his teeth each time he snarled and growled.

He was handsome, her brain told her and her body agreed, warming as he continued to stare at her. He had the same coloring as Michael but where her friend's features were almost pretty this man's were rougher, jagged. He was handsome in a more overtly masculine way than Michael, which she wouldn't have thought was possible if she hadn't been staring at it with her own eyes.

He was bigger than Michael. He'd beaten him in a fight. He'd attacked a Pack Alpha and won. The kind of power that hinted at made him dangerous on top of handsome and the fact that he kept staring at her and saying nothing but that one word, *mine*, sent a shiver of something terrifying through her veins.

Was it panic? She didn't think so. Fear? No. And that was the truly terrifying part. Because despite his show of violence and aggression, she was fighting her legs to keep from moving towards him. Worse, she didn't think it was *despite* those things at all. She thought it might actually be in part *because* he was so big and strong.

She had the strangest feeling that she was supposed to be at his side, not Michael's, but that couldn't be right.

"I didn't interfere." Michael was saying, "He did."

She cleared her throat, forced her gaze to her friend, "Michael, what's going on?"

He flickered a glance at her, his face softening with that look of concern again, "I'm sorry Zoey. I didn't think he'd find you here, not with your scent hidden among the entire pack. I tried to stop this. I've been trying to stop this all damn day."

"Stop what?" She asked in confusion and he reached for her but the second he touched her arm another snarl tore from the chest of the other man and she jerked away from her friend's touch.

Michael's touch felt... wrong, somehow. Not the comfort it had always been. Not causing that knot in her belly of need and despair. But she didn't have time to think about that because the other man snarled menacingly.

"Michael! I will rip your hands off and beat you to death with them if you touch what belongs to me again."

Michael growled right back, "Stop threatening me before you really piss me off Rafe."

"You want to fight me for her?" The other man's dark eyes lit gold again; his wolf showing through it was so close to the surface, "Let's fight *Alpha*. I'll beat you and then I'll take the girl and the pack. They were both supposed to be mine anyway."

Zoey felt her jaw fall open. Rafe. Michael had called him Rafe again. Add in what he'd just said about the pack being his and that meant he was exactly who she'd thought he was when she got that first good look at him.

Her mind was whirling, "Michael? What's going on? Tell me. Now. Because what my head is telling me can't possibly be right... can it?"

Michael sighed, started to reach for her again and then must have thought better of it considering the threat hanging in the air. He swiped his hand across his jaw instead. When he met her eyes again, there was more than just concern there this time. There was also a good portion of sadness.

"Zoey, you remember my brother?"

"Rafael." Her gaze automatically shifted back to him when Michael confirmed what she'd already put together, "Rafe."

That flash of recognition hit her again along with something else. It had been a long time. She'd barely been a teenager the last time she saw him. He'd taken off after the accident that took his parents life and the life of his twin brother, the same accident that had made Michael Alpha of the pack.

It was the something else that distracted her though, the thing that definitely hadn't been there when she'd known him before. The instant attraction to him was new. So was the urge to move towards him, to let him protect her, the belief that he was the one offering safety, comfort and home. None of that had been there when she'd known him before... before she'd turned eighteen, she realized.

Her head was still trying to figure out what that meant, how that was possible, when Michael's next words confirmed what her heart had been trying to tell her all day.

This was the important part. The impossible part. The part she never could have seen coming because it changed everything.

"He thinks you're his mate."

CHAPTER 4

afe Hudson was going to rip his little brother's intestines out and use them to choke him to death. It was a fantasy he'd been living over and over in his head for the past few hours. It was a fantasy that he would have fulfilled already if only *she* hadn't stopped him.

Her. Zoey. His mate. He was still trying to wrap his head around how that was even possible.

All of those years out there in the big, bad world. All of his time spent roaming from city to town to countryside. He hadn't been out there looking for her but he was what he was. He was a shifter and it was hard coded in him to seek the woman that was meant to make him whole. In the back of his mind, every time he encountered a new woman, a new wolf or other shifter, he'd wondered if she was the one.

He'd wondered if he would find her at his next stop or the one after that. He'd wondered where she was and if she was looking for him too. And, in his darkest moments, he'd wondered if fate had even seen fit to give him a mate when he'd already failed to protect those that meant the most to him once.

He'd failed his family, his entire pack. He had been the one to run past the boundary line. He was the one the hunters had followed back to camp. He was the reason they were all dead, every one of them.

His proud father, the leader of them all. His mother, the sweetest wolf to have ever been born. And Gabe, his littermate, his twin, his other half in every way. The only member of his family that hadn't been in the woods that day was Michael and because fate liked to throw punches when you were already down, Rafe knew that the reason his little brother hadn't been there was because he'd been with *her*.

Zoey.

To find out, after all of this time, that she was his? That she'd been his all along? That she was his but that she'd been here with *his brother*? Well, that was an injustice he wouldn't, and couldn't, tolerate.

Any other wolf being anywhere near her would have been enough to incite him to violence after he'd caught her scent. The fact that he'd scented her for the first time in his brother's home had been shocking but not altogether unrealistic. Michael had taken over the position of Pack Alpha, it was reasonable for him to have invited a member of the pack into his home. But her scent hadn't been casual or fleeting in Michael's home and that had been his first clue that something was wrong.

Her scent had been strong because she'd spent a lot of time there and realizing that his brother's scent and his mates were so closely intertwined had felt like the first blow in a fight he hadn't known was coming. Not at the time. Not until Michael purposefully tried to keep her from him, going so far as to refuse to tell him who the scent belonged to.

Rafe had left town after the attack on his family. He'd been injured, weak and damaged. He should have been dead. He'd wished he were dead. He'd known he was in no shape to take his rightful place at the head of the pack and he'd known what would happen if he stayed.

Somebody would have insisted Michael challenge him. The pack would have demanded it. He'd been weak and a Pack Alpha couldn't be weak. His little brother would have been next in line and he'd always been strong. He was the logical choice.

So Rafe had left. He'd refused to fight the only member of his family that was still alive for something he'd never wanted in the first place. Gabe was the one that had wanted to follow in their father's footsteps and lead. Not him.

Looking back, he could have simply stepped down. They probably would have let him. Nobody had wanted him as their leader then. A barely twenty-year-old Pack Alpha that was physically wounded and mentally unstable? No. They would have let him step down and stay but he hadn't wanted to stay.

He'd needed to get away. Get away from the people that stared at him, wondering how he'd survived when the other, stronger wolves hadn't. Get away from the little brother that kept telling him that it wasn't his fault, when Rafe knew that he was wrong. He'd just needed to get away from all the reminders of what he'd lost.

All he'd wanted was to live his life in peace, to mourn the loss of his family and find his mate, to have the chance to make a new family for himself, one he swore he would protect with his last breath if only fate would give him another chance.

He'd never have suspected that by giving up his life here he would be forfeiting years with the one woman that could make him whole again. He hadn't fought his brother to become Pack Alpha, to lead the pack or even for the right to the only home he'd ever known. But he would fight for this, for her.

She was his.

He growled again, or was still growling. He couldn't seem to control it. Every time he thought about her and Michael, he wanted to rip his brother apart with his teeth and his claws. He was barely holding his skin, his wolf scratching at the surface, willing Rafe to set him loose on anyone that dared keep his mate from him, even the brother they loved.

He hated that she was even standing next to his brother and seeing Michael touch her had ripped at the last shreds of humanity he'd been holding onto tonight. Maybe it had been stupid, definitely crazy, because the Sherriff was right. He could arrest him for the unprovoked attack. Worse, he could be subjected to pack punishment for attacking the Pack Alpha. But he hadn't cared then and he didn't care now.

If Michael touched her again, Rafe was going to launch himself across the small space and take his brother's throat.

His little brother. The only member of his family that was still alive. He should want to protect him, and he did, but that thought got all jumbled up with the anger and jealousy that had overtaken him when he realized that *his* mate was *Michael's* Zoey.

No. Not Michael's. She wasn't Michael's. She couldn't be. She was his and if he had to beat that truth into his little brother, then he would.

Zoey wouldn't like that, the little voice in the back of his head warned. He growled at the sliver of reason. She'd already stopped him once. She would try to do it again and he couldn't risk her jumping between them. His pride would be hurt if she tried to protect Michael over him but worse than that she could be physically hurt if she stepped between them.

She was human. Damn it, had he ever considered his mate being human? It felt like another cruel twist of fate. She wasn't supernatural which meant she was weak, frail, mortal. She could be hurt far too easily. She could die far too easily.

And he'd already lost too many people that were important to him.

A low moan filled the night air and it took him a moment to realize it was coming from him. It was a wolf's lament, his pain escaping the only way it could. And every wolf in the vicinity heard it and responded in kind.

A dozen people or more had piled through the back door of the lodge to see what was going on. The Sherriff was still standing between him and Michael, his head on a swivel, trying to keep an eye on both sides. His brother winced at the sound, his head tilting in recognition though his muscles remained tense and ready for the next attack.

He'd give Michael that. The boy had always been smart. Because Rafe might not have intended to let his grief emerge but now that it had, for just a split second there, he'd thought about using it to his advantage. If he moved quickly enough, he could drop Michael while he was distracted, grab his mate and run.

The thing that stopped him, again, was Zoey. She turned back to him at the sound of his moan. His mate's eyes met his and his heart pounded in his chest when she softened, worry filling her every feature, worry for him.

Automatically, she took a step in his direction and he started towards her. Magnets, that's what they were now that he'd scented her, and the need to be near her, to be with her, would only grow until he mated her. The need to claim her rode him hard and he knew that she was feeling the effects of the bond too.

She might be human but she'd been made for him. Her soul and his were two halves of the same and needed to be rejoined. She was itching to get to him too by now, the need to touch him, to put her scent on him as real as his need to have his on her. She might not know what it was, might think it was a simple spark of instant attraction, but it would grow into an all-consuming need as real and deep as his own.

It had already started.

He could see it in the way her eyes dilated when she looked him over. He could hear it in the increasing tempo of her heart rate. Her breaths were coming faster just from being near him and he needed to get them out of here, get them somewhere private, soon. Because he had a feeling if he scented her arousal here, in the open, he'd take her to the ground and seal their fate with his brother and half the pack watching them and damn the consequences.

He couldn't get over how damn pretty she was. He'd always thought she was pretty. Somewhere in the back of his mind, he'd noted the small, pale human that was always hanging around his brother was pretty and he remembered her clearly. But this woman, the one before him, wasn't that same girl. She'd grown up since he went away. It was like seeing her for the first time and she was the most beautiful creature he'd ever laid eyes on.

Her hair was a bright, coppery red. It tumbled down around her shoulders in soft curls and framed a face that promised sin and salvation. Her big green eyes were innocent but her full, red lips were made for seduction. She was a tiny little thing compared to him but he knew for a human she was about average height. There was nothing average about her body however. She had the kind of curves that should have come with warning signs and the red scrap of material she was wearing showed off miles of unblemished, porcelain skin.

Red. Red. Red. She was human but she'd lived among their kind since childhood. She knew what that color meant. She had to. It was an invitation at best and one he was willing to bet no member of the pack had missed, least of all his brother.

CHAPTER 5

Zoey took another step towards him. Michael reached out. Rafe growled the moment his brother's hand closed around her arm, jerking her to a stop.

He shoved the Sherriff and earned a few more feet up onto the bank when the older man stumbled backwards. Irrationally, he was already plotting the best way to take the Sherriff to the ground, the easiest way to rip out his brother's heart, and then the quickest route of retreat to get his mate out of here.

"Damn it Rafe. Don't make me put you down." The Sherriff put his hand near his weapon but he couldn't find it in himself to care, not when he heard his mate squeak loudly.

"Michael! Let go. He's hurting and I need to help!"

"What? No." His brother yelled right back. "You're not going anywhere near him. It isn't safe."

Rafe snarled at that. Safe? His little brother wanted to talk about safe? He had warned Michael once already not to touch his mate, not to get in the way.

Michael knew the rules. Pack Alpha or not, he couldn't interfere in a mate bond, not if it was uncontested by the two parties involved. He would be foolish to even try. A mated wolf was stronger than an unmated one and there was no reasoning with one in heat.

He would fight twice as hard. He would be twice as vicious. He wouldn't stop until he got to her, even if he had to put Michael in the ground to do it. His brother knew that.

The human part of his brain, the rational part of his brain, told him to think this through. He and Michael weren't littermates. He'd never been able to read him as well as he had Gabe. They weren't two pieces of the same puzzle but they were still brothers. They knew each other.

He knew Michael. Michael was always calm, always rational. He used his head and thought things through before he made a move.

Michael knew him. Rafe's strength came from emotion. He was action and gut instinct. He was the one that attacked first and asked questions later.

Michael knew him so Michael must know that he was tempting his own torture by touching the girl and yet, he'd done it anyway.

Why?

"Of course it's safe." Zoey scoffed, jerking her arm away from his brother, "You just said I'm his mate. If that's true, you know he would never hurt me."

Such trust in him, in their beliefs and traditions, made something new and warm take up residence in Rafe's chest. Attacking his own brother hadn't been the way to introduce her to any of this, to him, and probably hadn't won him any points. Still, she was fighting to get to him despite the road-block his brother presented.

Rafe watched them interact, tried to process what he was seeing. Ever since he'd walked into his brother's home earlier tonight, he'd been in a haze of lust and magic and rage. He hadn't stopped to think about much of anything except finding her but now that he had, he knew what it was he'd been missing.

She wasn't just a member of Michael's pack. She wasn't just a human that Michael liked and protected. She wasn't just Michael's friend. His brother loved her.

Somewhere, in the back of his mind, he'd known that. When he realized the scent of his mate belonged to the same girl that had been palling around with his brother since childhood, he'd known that. But at the same time, he'd thought that Michael was smarter than this.

Falling for a woman that wasn't his mate? For a woman that wasn't his? For a woman that his every instinct would demand he abandon when his true mate walked into his life?

It was childish and naïve and stupid, not things Michael had ever been. If Michael had fallen in love with her when they were children, before they'd known, that was one thing. But to have continued their relationship, knowing full well that they weren't fated, was cruel and heartbreaking... for them both.

Rafe thought about all of the signs he'd ignored earlier in the day. Her scent had been strong in Michael's home, as if she spent a lot of time there. And as soon as he'd scented her, Michael had known who she was but his brother refused to tell him, refused to help him find her, and so he'd raced out of the house alone, desperate to find her. Her scent had led him to her apartment and even there, in her tiny space, he'd still scented his brother.

They shared space. Their scents intertwined. He

should have put it together before but he'd been so consumed with the need to find her that his brain hadn't puzzled through the whole picture yet. Now, looking at them, the picture was still grainy and out of focus because it didn't make sense.

Their scents were all over each other's homes but they weren't all over each other. It was there, a light undercurrent that spoke to familiarity, but they hadn't been sleeping together. Michael's scent would have marked her if that were the case. And though his brother's scent lingered on her skin, that was as deep as it went, familiarity, ease, sporadic and random touches. It wasn't soul deep and for that, at least, he would let his brother keep his life.

Michael was in love with the girl but he hadn't taken her. He hadn't crossed that line. It raised a question he hadn't thought about earlier, one he didn't want to think about, one with an answer he was in no way prepared to hear.

Was she in love with Michael too?

He growled when he remembered the way they'd been looking at each other when he finally tracked her here, to the lodge. He'd been following her scent all over town for hours. Michael must have known that and taken advantage to get to her first. She'd been in his brother's arms when he arrived and if he hadn't interrupted...

He hated to even think it but if he'd been even ten seconds later and he'd found Michael kissing her, knowing full-well that she belonged to him, not even her sweet voice would have stopped him from beating his brother into the ground.

"Damn it Zoey. He's not stable. I'm trying to protect you." Michael got in her way again but saved himself another brutal attack by not touching her.

"From your brother?"

"He's not himself right now and neither are you. The mating heat... you don't want to do this. You'll regret it, when the magic wanes and the heat passes, you'll regret it and I care about you too much to let that happen."

Her chin jutted up, "You care about me?"

"You know I do." Michael lowered his voice, "I love you Zo."

Rafe snarled at the words. No. It was wrong. It was wrong in every way. Michael couldn't love her. She didn't belong to him. She was Rafe's mate. His.

"Mine!"

She glanced at him, her brows furrowing, before she looked back to his brother, "Michael, you don't get to say that now just because you think it will get you your way."

"That's not why I said it." Michael moved closer to her again, "You know me better than that."

Rafe growled. The Sherriff kept his hand on his weapon. The older man was getting jumpy. Even still, Rafe couldn't look away from his mate when she spoke again.

"You're right. I do know you and I know when you're lying so tell me the truth. Am I really his?"

"I don't know." Michael hedged, shot him a glance and earned another scowl, "Yeah, yeah I think you are."

"Jesus..." She sighed, ran a hand down her face, "This is a mess, just like you said."

"Zo..."

She glanced back up quickly, pain clear in her every feature, "Did you know? All this time, did you know?"

"No. God no."

"But you knew before you followed me out of the lodge didn't you? You knew and that's why you said all of those things about wanting to run away from your responsibilities and changing fate? You knew and you were keeping me from him? You're *still* keeping me from him."

Rafe could clearly hear the hurt in his mate's voice and from the way Michael reacted, so could he. His brother winced, his head lowering in a universal sign of apology. It was more than that though. Michael was Pack Alpha, he lowered his head to no one. But he did it, willingly, for this woman.

"She's mine. Let her go Michael." He snapped, impatient to end the connection his mate had to his brother, wanting to stomp it out now, now, now. "I'm not letting you keep her from me much longer brother."

"Don't let him near her." Michael didn't even look at him, only nodded at the Sherriff, "If he gets close to her, you take him down."

Rafe growled at the threat but before he could deliver another, or better yet, attack, his mate surprised him by laughing. It wasn't an amused laugh. It sounded near hysterical. He started to move towards her, noticed the Sherriff reaching for his gun and stopped. Michael started to reach for her as well, thought better of it and dropped his arm back to his side.

"Zoey?" Michael frowned.

"It's a little funny right?" She threw her hands up in the air, "I mean, for years you've told me that our connection was different. You told me that you loved me like a sister. *A sister!* And now it makes sense doesn't it? Your need to protect me and look after me? It's not because I'm yours. It's because I'm his."

Confusion circled him again as he tried to piece together the relationship his brother and his mate shared. Had Michael known she was fated to be with Rafe? She'd said their friendship was based on Michael's need to protect her, that he thought of her as a sister. He loved her, but was it possible that love was platonic? He hadn't touched her, not sexually, so Rafe had to hope so.

He might not like his little brother very much right now but he didn't want to break his heart. He didn't want to hurt him. Okay, maybe he did want to hurt him, badly, for daring to come between him and his mate, but he didn't really want to kill him.

Michael looked just as confused by her words. He also looked annoyed and frustrated. Rafe knew the look. He'd seen it on the face of his little brother only a handful of times. Usually, it had appeared when he realized he had lost. Something that had been rare even when they were pups.

Michael finally sighed, "Maybe."

"Maybe?" Rafe's little mate scoffed again. "Maybe I'm his. Maybe I'm not. But I'm definitely not yours so get out of my way Michael."

His brother winced as if she'd slapped him but kept his head, "No."

"You can't stop this!" She raised her voice, "If this is really happening, if this isn't some twisted nightmare, then there's nothing you can do to stop it, no matter how much either of us might wish you could."

"Zo..."

"No." She snapped when Michael said her name, "Don't Zo me like I'm the one being crazy here! This entire situation is crazy but I'm the only one acting reasonably. I'm the only one that's not fighting fate like I could possibly win."

"You're not fighting it because of the heat!" Michael yelled right back at her.

Rafe growled again. He didn't like the idea of anyone

raising their voice at his mate. His wolf was on a very short leash and he was about to gnaw through the last strands of it. He was trying to give them a second, to let them sort this out, mostly to keep from getting himself shot, but he wouldn't tolerate Michael yelling at her.

"I'm not fighting it because there's nothing to fight. This is fate. This is what we've been waiting for since the day I turned eighteen." Her lips trembled and her eyes watered, "It just happened with the wrong wolf."

Rafe really didn't like that. He didn't like that his mate looked close to tears. He didn't like that she was hurting. He really didn't like that she'd called him the wrong wolf. Did that make Michael the right one?

"Zoey?"

She sucked in a breath of air when he said her name for the first time and her eyes jerked back to his. Her eyes were the most beautiful mix of blue and green that he'd ever seen. He wanted to drown in them but not because there were tears there.

"Zoey, come here, come to me."

Michael growled and broke the moment when he stepped between them again, "Zoey, stop. Don't do this."

"You'll have to grab me again to stop me and I don't think that's a good idea."

She started to step around Michael again and Rafe thought, for just a second, that his smart, logical brother was going to do the right thing and let her go. He thought that Michael had realized he was fighting a losing battle. Whether he loved the girl or not, she wasn't his and rules were rules. Rafe had been the one that hated the rules, had bent them until they almost broke, but Michael had always played by them. Knowing that, he was shocked when he watched his brother anchor a hand around her wrist and jerk her to a stop once again.

"Michael! No!" She yelped.

Rafe growled, his feet moving before he'd consciously decided that he was done waiting and watching. His fist connected with the Sherriff's gut, doubling him over, and he moved easily around him. He had a momentary flash of his mate's eyes going wide but he jerked his attention off of her and put the full brunt of his weight behind it when he swung at Michael this time. He connected with his brother's jaw, snapping his head around, but he didn't wait to see if Michael regained his balance for an attack.

He swept his mate into his arms in one easy move and headed up the hill. A sense of rightness immediately settled over him, calming the worst of his anger. She was his and she was here, in his arms. He could keep her safe now. He would claim her and then the terrible wave of jealousy he was feeling would ease and they could talk about all of this rationally tomorrow. After he'd mated her so that they were tied together forever.

"Rafe!"

He smiled when she yelled his name this time. Yes, that sounded better. That sounded right. It was his name that should always be on her lips. Only his.

"Rafe, wait!"

"Can't. Done waiting." He started to shift her into a more comfortable position to run when he felt the sting in his back. "Dammit no!"

The pain radiated out as if he'd been stung by a thousand bees all at once. He took one more step. Two. His legs felt weak and the world shifted on its axis. He had the forethought to understand his body was failing, that he was going to fall, and he held his fragile, breakable mate to his chest, trying to shield her and protect her.

His knees hit the ground first and he winced at the jarring collision, "They can't take you from me. You. Are. Mine."

His mate opened her mouth to respond but only a shriek came out because his back gave and he slumped forward. He tried to shield her from the enormity of his body weight but it was no use. He landed on top of her as gently as he could considering he could barely move his limbs. There was a strange sense of accomplishment having her pinned beneath him and his heart thumped at the close-ness, at the fact that their skin was touching, that their scents were mixing, even as his body failed and his vision wavered.

"What's wrong? Oh God, what's happening?"

He used the last of his strength to brush her hair back off her face. Pretty. So pretty. She reminded him of the girl from that story, the one with the big, bad wolf. He smiled at the thought, tried to file it away to tell her later, certain she would laugh because he was exactly that.

"Why are you smiling?" She tried to wiggle beneath him but it was useless, she wasn't getting free of him that easily, "Oh, hell, you're as crazy as he said you were aren't you?"

"Not crazy." He dropped his head, his heavy head, against the curve of her neck and breathed in her sweet, distinctive scent, "Yours. I'm yours."

"Lucky me."

He thought he sensed sarcasm in her tone and smiled again. Feisty. His mate was feisty. She'd argued with her Pack Alpha, gone toe-to-toe, and she'd won. She would handle him too, he had no doubt. They were going to be a good pair.

"Mine."

She snorted, '"Yeah, you mentioned that."

Her soft hand brushed his hair back off his forehead and he closed his eyes and enjoyed the touch. He couldn't open them again. Darkness closed in all around him. He was going under. He knew the feeling. It wasn't the first time he'd been shot after all. Luckily, it wasn't a bullet this time. His only regret was that he hadn't been able to get her away, get her somewhere safe, because when he was unconscious, he wouldn't be able to protect her.

"Rafe?" Her voice, sweet with concern for him again.

"I'll find you." He mumbled the promise, unsure if his words even made sense through the fog of the drugs in his system. "They can't keep me from you. I'll find you."

The world shifted away and the warmth of the drugs lulled him into sleep. He hated sleep. He only ever dreamed in nightmares. Flashes of pain and agony, destruction and loneliness. But this time was different, because he had his mate in his arms, underneath him, her body pressed to his, her scent in his nose. And just before he went under completely he thought he heard her say something that would have made him smile again, if only he were coherent.

"You won't have to. I'm not going anywhere."

CHAPTER 6

Zoey was trapped under two hundred plus pounds of pure, unadulterated werewolf. She should have been screaming her head off. She should have been struggling to get away from him. She should have been fighting it but she'd already figured out that fighting was impossible.

Her senses had betrayed her and her body wasn't far behind.

She reveled in the smell of him. Man and musk, pine and dirt. She ached at the feel of him. Hard muscles and coiled strength. And she wanted more of it, wanted all of it, now. Some voice deep inside of her was whispering that he was hers and she could, and should, do whatever she damn well pleased to him, conscious or not.

She whimpered when the still slightly rational part of her brain forced her to squirm, trying to free herself, but in effect all it did was rub her body against his and make pinwheels of desire swirl in her blood. She should have been trying to get away. Instead, it was all she could do not to wrap her legs around his waist and rock herself against him. She gave in to the urge to wrap her arms around him, to hold him close to her, cradle him and try to offer some semblance of comfort, even as her head screamed at her that this was wrong, all wrong.

These weren't her feelings. They couldn't be. This was the heat. It was the mating bond taking over and wresting control from her.

This was Rafe. Michael's *brother*. A man she hadn't seen in years. A wolf that, last she'd heard, was still completely unbalanced from the horrors he'd faced when he watched most of his family murdered in front of him.

Had she cared about him before, when she was just a girl? Maybe. Probably. But in all honesty, she didn't remember. He hadn't been a part of her life, not really. She had vague memories of Gabe teasing her good-naturedly about her crush on his little brother. Remembered Rafe teasing Michael not so good-naturedly about it.

Had he known back then? Impossible. She'd been too young. But was it possible that he'd felt... something? Just as Michael had felt something for her all of these years that he hadn't been able to explain, something that told him to protect her like she was family, because one day, she would be?

Michael.

Her senses came jolting back to her. Not even the magical heat that drew her to Rafe could mask the conflicting emotions she was feeling when it came to her best friend now. Confusion, frustration and more than a little bit of anger. They weren't new emotions where he was concerned but they were all amplified now to a level she couldn't possibly ignore or swallow down like she'd been doing for years.

"Michael!"

"I'm coming Zo! I'm coming!" He staggered into her view, rubbing a jaw that was already turning an array of colors as his impressive genetics fought to heal him, "Are you okay?"

"Never been better."

"Yeah, I know. Stupid question." He winced and shot a look over his shoulder, "Wiley, help me get him off her."

She bit the inside of her cheek to keep from hissing at him when he grabbed Rafe by the shoulder and started to haul him up. She couldn't force her hands to let go of him until Michael frowned, looked between them and uttered a growl of his own. She swallowed a whine and let her friend and the Sheriff roll her unconscious mate off of her.

Her mate. She was Rafe's mate. He was hers.

She could feel the truth in the statement. She'd felt it even before she'd known what was going on. That urge to go to him, to be with him, the immediate and intense attraction she'd felt, they'd all been signs. She'd heard the mated females in the pack talk about the bond, about the heat, she just hadn't expected it to be so instantaneous or so complete.

She hadn't expected Rafe.

If it had been Michael, she would have known how to handle it. She would have known what to do. She would have leaped into his arms and never looked back. Her head and her heart and the heat would all have been in perfect, blissful harmony and everything would have been right in the world. She wouldn't have second-guessed herself for even a minute.

But it wasn't Michael. It had never been Michael. It was never going to be Michael.

Hadn't she been trying to get that through her thick skull earlier tonight?

She'd come outside to get some fresh air, to get some space from him, but he'd followed her. He'd touched her and talked to her and she'd started to think that he was coming around to the idea of them being together, even though she knew better. Even though she knew that she wasn't his mate. Even though she knew that he knew that.

Looking back on it, the moment felt as if it had happened a lifetime ago. It was a faded, foggy memory already. Indistinct. Important only because it had been the last one she'd had with Michael before her entire world shifted, until it realigned, and he was no longer the center of it.

Rafe was.

The others rolled him to his side and she sucked in a breath of air now that she wasn't being smothered. She missed him. Instantly. Missed his weight and the heat of his body, and she reached for him before she'd made a conscious decision to move.

She rolled up to sitting, ignored the hand Michael offered her, and felt for a pulse in Rafe's neck. It was there. Slow. Far too slow for a shifter. His chest was rising and falling softly but he didn't so much as twitch when she swiped his hair off his forehead and trailed her hand across his cheek. The jolt of electricity that flowed through her when they touched skin-to-skin was powerful but he didn't react at all.

She frowned, "Something's wrong with him."

"There's a lot of things wrong with him."

She hissed in a breath at Michael's grumble and spun to face him. He was standing at her feet, close enough to touch, and for the first time in as long as she could remember, she didn't feel the urge to reach out for him. Considering the anger she felt rising inside of her, that didn't surprise her. What surprised her was the urge to lash out at him, to put herself between him and his brother, and not to protect Michael but to protect Rafe.

"What happened? What did you do to him? If you hurt him in any way, I will..."

"You will what? You're going to threaten me now too?" Michael scoffed, "I was trying to protect you Zo!"

"What did you do?" She heard her voice rise an entire octave about the same time she saw Michael's eyes widen in shock and horror.

She'd never yelled at him before. Ever. She'd been angry with him plenty of times. They'd been friends too long for them not to argue, not to fight, but she'd never screamed at him. She'd never even wanted to. Until now.

"Easy there..." Wiley stepped between the two of them, holding his hands out in her direction as if she might go into full-attack mode, "He didn't do anything. Calm down Zoey."

She turned her anger on the older man, "Tell me what's wrong with Rafe!"

"Nothing's wrong with him. He's just sleeping off the drugs."

"The drugs?"

"Yeah." Wiley shrugged, "I tranqued him."

She sucked in a shocked gulp of air and then winced and stared down at her hands. She'd curled her hands into fists so hard that her nails were cutting into her skin. She consciously uncurled her fingers and fought off the urge to swing her fist at the Sheriff's head.

"You did what?" She hissed through her teeth.

"Tranqued him."

"Why would you do that?" She struggled between keeping her eyes on the men that had already hurt her mate and turning her full attention back on Rafe to check that he was still breathing.

"Because I told him to." Michael spoke up.

Vaguely, she remembered his words from earlier, when they'd been facing off and she hadn't even known what was happening. Michael had told the Sheriff that if Rafe went anywhere near her to take him down. She remembered thinking that the Sheriff didn't stand a chance of taking Rafe in a fight. She hadn't realized they weren't planning to fight fair.

"Why?"

"Why?" Michael growled, his face twisting into a menacing scowl, "Why? The fact that you're even asking me is proof that you're not thinking clearly."

She wasn't thinking clearly. She knew that. Every single thought she had was being processed through a new filter. Rafe.

How did it affect Rafe? How did she get to Rafe? How did she protect Rafe? How did she get Rafe back? And how long would it be until she could have his skin against hers again, his body pressing into hers and sealing the bond once and for all?

"Jesus, Zoey! You're not even listening to me."

She snapped back to attention and felt a blush steal over her cheeks when Michael frowned at her. He knew where her thoughts had gone. It was clear from the disapproval on his face that he knew exactly what she had been thinking. Even still, she couldn't shut it off.

There was an invisible link between her and Rafe now and it was only getting stronger. Attraction had flickered to life as soon as she saw him, but it was more than that. She'd fought to get to him, felt the urge to be closer to him, and her body had responded to him fighting for her too. Then he'd grabbed her, touched her for the first time, and it was like a piece of herself that she'd never known was missing fell into place.

She glanced back at Michael and her heart squeezed too tight in her chest. It hurt, but not in the way it had for four years. She stared at his handsome face, but objectively, for possibly the first time ever. He was good-looking, too good-looking really, but her heart didn't skitter and race at the mere sight of him now.

Her attraction to him was gone. Her mind whirled as she tried to figure out how that was possible. He was just as handsome as he had been a half hour ago. He was still her best friend.

She still loved him, that hadn't gone anywhere. Love like that didn't just disappear. But it was different now, looking at him and knowing that he had been right before, when he'd said that being together would have felt wrong because they didn't belong together.

She hadn't understood it at the time. She hadn't understood it today. Not until the moment her eyes had met Rafe's and she'd felt the beginning of that bond take root somewhere deep inside her, could she have ever understood the difference in loving someone and being mated.

She didn't love Rafe. She wasn't delusional enough to believe a magical bond could make that happen instantaneously. She did believe that it was possible for her to fall in love with him though, because otherwise, what was the point? The bond was only the beginning, not the end goal like she'd always thought it was.

This was just the beginning for them.

CHAPTER 7

"Zoey!"

"What?" She snapped when Michael growled her name again.

"I said you need to back off him. Wiley's going to take him down to the station and lock him up so he can't hurt you or anyone else until we get all of this figured out."

She gaped at him, "You can't be serious."

"Of course I'm serious."

"There are so many things wrong with what you just said I don't even know where to start."

"I'm Alpha of this pack, Zoey. You can question me. You can disagree with me all you want, but it's my decision to make and I've already made it. He's getting locked up for the night."

She'd never seen Michael like this and she found herself staring. She thought she knew every side of him. She'd been his best friend since she was ten years old. But she'd never seen him take a stand and be wrong and that was what he was doing.

He was wrong. Maybe for the first time ever. Michael

was wrong about all of it. He was Pack Alpha because Rafe had left. He ruled over the pack but he wasn't a dictator. And he had no right to interrupt or stop them from sealing the mate bond.

Rationally, she knew why he was doing it. All of the cocksure arrogance was to hide the weakness he felt when it came to her and their complicated relationship. He needed to assert his power because this was something he couldn't control. And she thought that maybe, just maybe, some part of him hated the idea of losing her, because earlier, on the shoreline of the river where they'd carved their names as silly kids, he'd looked at her and told her that fate had gotten it all wrong and she should have been his.

He'd known then. He'd all but admitted it. He'd known then that she didn't belong to him, didn't belong with him but he'd touched her and she was certain, still, maybe more so, that he'd been going to kiss her before Rafe tackled him to the ground.

He'd known that his brother was coming for her, some-how, he had figured it out, and he hadn't warned her. He hadn't told her. Instead, he'd declared that she should have been his. He'd said that he was going to fix it, fix this, and that memory slithered slow and uneasy through her until a knot formed in her stomach.

Fix it? Fix fate? Fix the bond she felt to Rafe? How was Michael planning to do that? By keeping them apart? By keeping Rafe locked up so he couldn't get to her? If she fought, would he knock her out too? How far was he willing to go to fix what he saw as a problem?

Zoey licked her lips, darting a glance down at her mate, and made the decision. It was the only one she could make. If they kept fighting, she would say something she couldn't take back. Michael would do something they'd never be able to come back from. And she couldn't, wouldn't, walk away from Rafe, not now, not ever. So she had to find another way.

She took a step back. It almost killed her. Every instinct in her body hissed at her to stop, to turn around, to stay close to Rafe and protect him, but she held her hands up and put some space between them. She stepped backwards until her unconscious mate lay between them, her at his head and Michael at his feet.

"Okay."

Michael's eyes narrowed suspiciously, "Okay?"

"You're right. You're Pack Alpha. If you think Rafe needs to be locked up tonight, then there's nothing I can do to stop you."

Michael stared at her for a long moment. She could feel him picking through her brain, trying to figure out what her motives were. He was smart and a good leader and he knew her better than anyone.

She was more surprised than she probably had a right to be when his shoulders sagged with relief and he nodded. He'd accepted her white flag too easily. He expected her to still side with him, like she always had on everything. But she wasn't that same girl anymore. She loved Michael but Rafe was her mate. He came first now.

"Good." He sighed, rubbed at his jaw, and then sighed again, "Thank you."

"For what?"

"For trusting me." He tried for a smile but it didn't take, "I promise I'm going to do everything I can to fix this Zoey."

The fear and panic that she'd been expecting from the moment she realized what was happening finally made an appearance. Something dark twisted her guts and she clenched her fists again and bit her tongue to keep from lashing out at Michael. He wasn't trying to hurt her, she told herself. He was trying to help. The problem of course was that for the first time, he didn't know what she needed at all. He didn't know what she was thinking. Because as far as she was concerned, there was nothing to fix.

Her body. Her heart. Her soul. She belonged to Rafe and that knowledge was undeniable.

She swallowed past the lump in her throat, "I do trust you Michael. I trust you to do the right thing."

His gaze flickered over her, that mix of remorse and sadness, but he didn't respond. If he understood what she'd really been saying, he didn't let on. He simply stared at her for a long moment and then nodded, as if he was having an internal debate and he'd just decided something important. When he spoke again, she realized she'd been right.

"You should go on home."

Her jaw fell open, "What?"

"Go home. Take a shower. Get changed. I'll deal with this mess and then I'll come over and we can talk about all of this."

"No."

"I need to get him moved before he rouses, Zo."

"Fine. I'll help you. But I'm not leaving him." She put her hands on her hips and glared at him.

"You think I'd hurt my own brother?"

"Well, you did just have him shot."

"Tranqued. There's a difference." He glowered.

"Really? You think he's going to see it that way when he wakes up?" She raised a skeptical eyebrow, "You shot your brother. Your brother that barely survived a gunshot wound once before. Your brother that witnessed your parents being shot and killed with his own eyes. Do you really think he's going to differentiate between being shot with a bullet and being shot with a dart when he comes to or do you think he's just going to be even more pissed off than he already was?"

As she spoke, she watched her words sink in and hated herself for them. She hated herself for bringing up the worst day of Michael's life. For making him remember his loss, as if it ever really faded from his mind. She hated that she had to point out that shooting Rafe had been a mistake because the Michael she knew, kind, thoughtful, practical Michael, should have known the torture his brother had lived with better than anyone.

But he hadn't been thinking when he gave that order for the Sheriff to shoot Rafe.

He hadn't looked at him and seen his brother. He'd only looked at him and seen a threat. To her. To them. To what they had.

And she didn't blame him. There were plenty of women she'd hated on sight alone because she'd thought they might be the one meant for Michael. In another time and place, hell, even earlier tonight, Michael's simple, knee-jerk reaction to protect her, to keep her for himself, whatever his reasons, would have come off as impossibly sweet in her romantic mind.

Now she only wished that Michael hadn't been present at all when Rafe came for her. If she'd been alone, none of this would have happened. If Michael hadn't followed her outside, he wouldn't have thought he had to defend her, jumped between them or issued orders to have his brother shot and then imprisoned.

Her stomach knotted again. How were they going to come back from this? Rafe and Michael? Their relationship had already been strained. It had been fraught with tension even with miles of space between them. The pack was rightfully Rafe's by birth but he'd given it to Michael without a fight. He'd left town.

Why had he come back now? And what did it mean that his first night here he and Michael were rolling on the ground, fighting with tooth and claw, over her? Worse, she couldn't help but wonder if Rafe would give her up to his brother as easily as he'd given up his pack.

No. She shook the thought away. No, he wouldn't have fought Michael if he hadn't wanted her for himself. She was his mate. He'd said so himself. He'd also said that he was hers.

It was a distinction that warmed her heart, maybe because she was human and she wasn't promised some pre-destined soulmate or maybe because she'd just always wanted someone to call her own. Whatever it was, whatever had made fate decide they would be a good pair, she wanted a chance at it, with Rafe.

"He'll understand why I did it after he calms down." Michael didn't sound convinced.

"How long do you think that's going to take? For the heat to pass I mean?" She shrugged as if it wasn't the most pressing thing on her mind.

"Until after the full moon." Michael swiped a hand through his hair, "It won't ever go away, not completely, but if I can keep you two apart until after tomorrow night, it'll buy us some time to come up with a plan."

"A plan?"

"To break the bond."

She bit her tongue. There were too many questions rolling around inside of her and if she got started now, she might never finish. Besides, if Michael answered wrong, she was likely to punch him. Something she didn't want to do. So she didn't ask him why he was so set on breaking the bond, on keeping them apart, she only nodded and moved back to Rafe.

She brushed his unruly hair off his forehead again. He twitched. He leaned his face into her touch and she covered a smile. He would be awake soon. Strong werewolf man, they'd tranqued him and still couldn't keep him down.

She remembered his last words to her. He'd said that he would find her. She knew that he would. If she took Michael's advice and went home and showered and changed, Rafe would wake up in that cell alone and he'd break every bone in his body trying to get to her. So she wasn't going to let him wake up alone. She wasn't going to make him find her. Because she wasn't leaving his side.

"Come on, I'll help you get him up."

Michael frowned, "I don't think you should touch him any more than completely necessary."

She almost rolled her eyes. Touching was part of the bond, the bond he intended to break. She could tell him that it was completely necessary for her to be touching Rafe right now but she had a feeling that would get her a personal escort home, in the other direction of the police station, so she simply nodded and raised her hands.

"Okay."

Michael nodded, "Wiley? Grab his shoulders."

"Where are we taking him?" The older man was still scowling at all of them like they were errant children.

"To the station."

"I meant, the car..."

"I'll pull my SUV around." She offered and then shrugged when Michael stared at her, "I'm not tossing him in the back of your truck like a bag of garbage. There's plenty of room in my Jeep. I'll pull it around so you don't have to carry him so far."

"Fine." Michael nodded after several long moments, "But after that, you're going home."

She snorted, "Like hell I am."

"Zo, I'm not arguing with you about this again."

"Good, because you'll lose. Again." She headed towards the back porch and groaned when she realized half the pack was still crowding around watching them, "Everybody enjoying the show?"

The whispers hushed and they moved out of her way. She grabbed her purse from where she'd left it and headed through the lodge to the front to retrieve her Jeep. This was going to be big news among the pack, among the whole town. And she was certain it was already spreading like wildfire.

Rafe was back. He'd attacked Michael. And he'd claimed the woman they all thought belonged to their Pack Alpha as his own.

She'd been right. Something powerful was in the air tonight. And it changed everything.

CHAPTER 8

His head hurt like a son-of-a-bitch. Rafe struggled to sit upright. His muscles screamed in protest and everything ached. He squinted in the fluorescent-lit room and growled as his surroundings began to make sense.

Concrete walls. Concrete floors. A metal cot with a bare mattress and an open toilet in the corner.

"Son of a..." Rafe dropped his head into his hands and scrubbed at his face.

His brother had thrown him into a jail cell. The little shit. He'd had the sheriff tranq him and while he was out they'd thrown him in a cell. Bastards. He hadn't done anything wrong. Nothing except try to claim his mate. Michael was the one that had gotten in the way. Michael was the one that had interfered. He should be the one in this cell but of course he wasn't. Because Michael was Pack Alpha.

Rafe's head hurt too bad to even think about how that was his own doing. How he was the one that should have been Pack Alpha. Should have been making the decisions.

Should have spent the past few years creating a life and a family with his mate instead of roaming the country alone with no place to call home.

His mate. Zoey. The fog that had been clouding his skull cleared at the thought of her. Zoey. *His* Zoey.

He could smell her. It was faint but there. The sweet scent of vanilla and cinnamon. His woman's scent. He'd know it anywhere. He sniffed his clothes and smiled softly. He was covered in her scent but that wasn't where it was coming from. That was mixed with his already, just the way he wanted it.

The scent his nose had picked up on was something else. Something that made his blood hot and his fists curl. Zoey's scent mixed with someone else's. Mixed with Michael's.

He swallowed a growl and lunged at the bars. He needed out of here. Now. A cell couldn't hold him, not when he was determined to get to his mate.

Only as soon as his hands closed on the bars he hissed in pain and jerked back as if he'd been burned. No, not as if. He stared down at the welts on his palms and growled again. Silver. The bars of the cell were reinforced with silver. The one metal that could harm a wolf. He cursed his brother all over again. Of course Michael would think of installing silver into the bars of the cells at the local jail. He'd always been smart and a pain in the ass.

Rafe swiped his hands on his shirt and retreated to the bunk. He couldn't escape. Couldn't get out. Not on his own.

He tried to focus on his other senses. He could smell Zoey. She was somewhere nearby. So was Michael and someone else. The Sheriff maybe? He couldn't be sure. His ears pricked and he could pick up bits and pieces of the conversation they were having upstairs.

A smile nudged at his mouth as he listened in. Zoey. His sweet, fiery mate was yelling. Not just yelling but yelling at Michael. She was yelling at the Alpha of the pack. For him. But his smile faded as he listened to his brother yelling right back at her.

A growl hung in his throat. Michael had no right. None. He didn't get to yell at Zoey. He didn't get to keep them apart. But stronger than the anger was the worry he felt building inside of him. His mate was challenging the Pack Alpha and Rafe wasn't there to protect her because he'd handled everything all wrong and gotten himself locked up.

He needed out of this cell. Now. Silver or no silver. His mate needed him.

He knew that Michael had feelings for Zoey. His brother wouldn't harm her. Not on purpose. But at some point, he would have to stand up to her. Because he was Pack Alpha. He would have to show his strength and shut her down. And Rafe couldn't, and wouldn't, let his brother punish her for defending him.

Instead of trying to pry the bars open again, he went to the small window. The bars there were probably laced with silver too so he didn't bother. He focused on the concrete blocks instead. With a whole lot of energy, he might be able to punch his way through but that tranquilizer had weakened him. It would take too long and he didn't know how much time he had left before someone came to check on him or…

The sound of footsteps behind him had him spinning back towards the front of the cell. He was prepared for the worst. For another tranquilizer from that bastard Sherriff or for his brother. He hadn't been prepared to see *her* on the other side though and relief squeezed his heart.

"Zoey." He rushed towards him and only caught himself a moment before he touched the bars.

"Shh, they'll hear us." She hushed as she moved towards him quickly now. "I snuck away but we don't have long until they realize I'm not in the bathroom."

All of his aches and pains disappeared with her nearness. The only thought in his head was how to get closer to her. He needed to touch her, feel her, taste her.

She looked beautiful. She would always look beautiful to him. Because she was his.

But he couldn't help the snarl that tore from his throat when he caught a whiff of his brother's scent coming from her. He scowled She was still wearing that tiny, slip of a red dress that made his wolf salivate but she had a thin hunter-green jacket with the gold emblem of the Sherriff's station on the sleeve pulled over it, as if she'd gotten cold. The jacket. It was Michael's. And he wanted to gut his brother for giving it to her to wear when he must have known how it would rile Rafe.

"What's wrong?" She whispered as she curled her fingers over the bars of the cage he was trapped in. "You don't look happy to see me."

"That jacket." He spit through gritted teeth. "Take it off. Now."

Her brows furrowed and she looked at the jacket, "What? Wh..."

"Now. Zoey. Take it off or I swear I'm going to rip it off you." He watched her eyes flare with recognition and heat, "It smells like my brother and you should only, ever, smell like me. Take. It. Off."

She bit her lip and her cheeks flushed the prettiest shade of pink. She shrugged her shoulders and the jacket slid to the floor. He groaned when she followed the order and his blood boiled hot for another reason. She'd followed his command, taken off the offending article of clothing, and on top of that now he could see so much more of her pale, porcelain skin.

His. She was his. And the heat was going to his head being this close to her.

"Come here." He ordered.

Still biting her lip, she edged against the bars, "Rafe..."

"Say it again." He whispered, pressing as close to her as he could without burning his skin.

"Rafe..." She stifled a moan when he traced her fingers with his own, a shudder running through them both, "Rafe, this is crazy. I... oh God, it's like lightning in my veins."

"I know." He lifted her hand, pulling it closer so he could scent her right at the pulse in her wrist.

He knew what she meant. This entire situation was crazy. The two of them. The heat. The problem that Michael posed as Pack Alpha, trying to keep them apart. But craziest of all was how intense the heat was, the need to have her, to possess her. He craved her more than the air in his lungs.

"You're mine." He dragged his teeth across her pale wrist, "You're mine, Zoey."

"Yours." She moaned almost incoherently. "I'm yours."

"Not yet you're not. But you will be." He licked her and the taste made his wolf howl, "Need you."

"Yes."

Ignoring the bite of pain, he reached through the bars and wound a hand in her hair. He tilted her face up and pressed his lips to hers. The silver burned his cheek where he couldn't avoid the bars of his cell but it didn't matter. Nothing did. Not when he finally, finally had the taste of his mate on his lips.

Sweet, so sweet. Her taste seeped inside of him and started a riot in his bloodstream. Her lips were soft and sweet and when they met his, it felt like a piece of the puzzle he'd always been missing slid into place.

How had he lived without this? All this time? All these years? And his mate had been right here, waiting for him.

Rafe groaned and licked at her lips. Zoey made a small sound that made his wolf purr as she opened to him. Her tongue met his, warm, wet velvet. He sucked and she whimpered again. He pressed closer, needing more, so much more, but the burn of the silver cut at him and he winced away.

Zoey was gasping for breath when he released her and it took everything inside him not to reach for her again. Her cheeks were rosy and her lips were red. Her green eyes were glassy. But she blinked and they cleared as swiftly as the color left her cheeks.

"Oh my God! Rafe!" She reached through the bars and gently stroked his burned cheek, "What happened? That wasn't there earlier."

He winced as he felt his cheek already beginning to heal, "It's the bars. They're laced with silver. They weaken my wolf and burn me if I touch them."

"Oh my God! Rafe!" She hissed with a roll of her eyes, "Why didn't you say something?"

"It wouldn't have mattered. I needed to touch you. Taste you. And I can't get out of here."

"Seriously? You underestimate me just like your brother does." She huffed and bent to retrieve the jacket from the floor, rifling in the pockets, "It has to stop. I can't deal with the both of you being alpha, chauvinist assholes."

"Zoey..." He started but he snapped his mouth shut when she stood back up and jangled a keyring at him. "Oh."

"Yeah. Oh." She smirked, "I stole the keys before I snuck down here. I could've let you out earlier if you'd told me that the bars hurt you. It's called communication. If we're going to be mates..."

"We *are* mates." He growled.

"Then you're going to have to tell me how all of this works. Not a wolf, remember? Just a human."

He grinned as he watched her work through the set, searching for the right key. His mate was incredible. He'd already known she was beautiful. She was also smart and feisty and absolutely perfect for him. Fate had gotten it right no matter what his brother thought.

"Not for long."

"What?" She glanced up at him from beneath thick lashes as she slipped another key into the slot and it clicked.

"You won't just be human for long." He slid through the door of the cell as soon as she opened it and pulled her into his arms, nuzzling her neck and taking in as much of her scent as he could, "You'll be a wolf once I bite you."

She moaned and tilted her head back, giving him full access to her neck and shivering, "Rafe, please..."

"No." He forced himself to pull back.

"But..."

"No." He nipped at her lush lips and then met her glassy gaze again, "Not here. Not now. Not like this. I've waited too long for you and you're not making that decision in the heat of the moment."

He could take her without biting her. He hoped. He would have to control his wolf and the bastard that lived inside of him was snapping at the chance to sink his teeth into her. But Rafe wouldn't let him. Not now. Not yet. He didn't trust his wolf not to hurt her.

More than that, he didn't trust her to make the decision

with the heat bearing down on them. She'd said all of this was crazy. He knew it was. Fast and crazy and out of control, and he couldn't let his wolf near her. Not like that.

When he bit her, when he marked her and gave her a wolf of her own, made her like him and sealed the bond, it wouldn't be in the heat of the moment.

He would take her. Claim her with his human half. But he wouldn't bite her. Not tonight. He could control his wolf. He could keep himself reined in. He could and he would. It had been a long time since he'd been on the same page as his wolf but on this, they would have to agree and he would have to win.

Because she was his world now and he wouldn't let anything hurt her.

"Rafe..."

"We have to get out of here." He reminded her when he realized they were still rubbing against each other, scenting one another, marking each other the only way they could, with their scents. "Before they come for me."

Zoey nodded quickly, "Michael wants to stop this."

"Michael doesn't get to decide this." He growled. "You decide. Do you want this? Me? Do you trust that fate got it right?"

She met his eyes. Those beautiful blue-green and gold-flecked eyes weren't glassy anymore. They were steady and full of heat and desire. And something else, something that looked like trust.

"Yes." She answered without hesitation.

CHAPTER 9

Rafe couldn't let go of her. He held her hand or rather, she held his as she dragged him down the hallway towards the emergency exit door. She'd reassured him she had the key that wouldn't set off any alarms and as she pushed the door open he felt another surge of pride. Sneaky little mate.

They emerged from underground into a back alley. It was dark. No lights from the street reached here. Nothing but moonlight and it made his wolf scratch at his skin.

He wanted out. Wanted to play with his mate. Wanted to claim her.

Rafe took a deep breath and let it out slowly. He forced his wolf back down. Not yet. He was in control, not the wolf. He had to stay in control. It wasn't about his screwed-up head and his scarred memories. This was about Zoey, his mate, and he wouldn't put her at risk by letting his near feral wolf near her, not while the heat was so powerful.

"Where are we going?" He managed as he followed behind her up the narrow alley. "Your place?"

"No way. That's the first place Michael will look for us." Zoey scoffed.

"Well, since my brother took both the Hudson house and the pack lodge, I don't exactly have a place for us to go, babe."

Zoey stopped suddenly and spun to face him, "Did you just call me babe?"

He froze, unsure of what to say. Was that a bad thing? A good thing? He couldn't tell at first but then he saw it. He saw the twinkle in her eyes. The way her mouth just slightly tipped upward at one corner. He grinned.

"Yeah." He used his grip on her hand to pull her closer, "Yeah, I did." He lowered his head and nuzzled her neck again, "And you like it."

"Mmm." She moaned when he licked her pulse and he groaned as her taste swarmed him again.

In two steps, she was up against the brick wall. He pinned her in place with his big body. She fit perfectly against him. All of her curves molded to him in all the best ways. He was hard and she was so soft. He rubbed his aching length against her and she moaned his name again.

God he loved that sound.

"Rafe, please..."

"Zo, baby..." He groaned as she wrapped her arms around him and opened her legs wider, letting him notch himself between them. "We have to..." He hissed when her warm heat rubbed up and down his length as her dress rucked up, "Fuck."

"Yes."

His head was foggy again and Rafe knew there was something they were supposed to be doing. Her. He wanted to do her. His mate. Zoey. She was his and nobody could keep her from him. The thought pierced his subconscious and he forced himself to pull back from her despite every cell in his body rejecting the very idea.

Michael wanted to keep her from him.

"We have to go somewhere." He reminded her when she made the most adorable pouting face, "Somewhere far from here, where Michael won't think to look for us. Where can we go, baby? Think."

Zoey chewed her bottom lip, "Uh, I... um, the cabin at the lake?"

He nodded as soon as the words left her pretty lips. The cabin. He'd forgotten about the cabin. It had been so long since he'd been there. Since the summer before the hunters took everything from him. He and Gabe had bought it together, intending to fix it up, but they'd never gotten the chance. Gabe had died and...

No. He shook off the pain that came with that thought. This wasn't the time. If he got lost in his head now, he'd put Zoey at risk and he couldn't do that. He wouldn't do that. If he didn't get them out of here, now, he'd lose Zoey too. Not the same way he'd lost Gabe but he would lose her all the same. Michael would take her from him. Keep her from him. He had to get them out of here and he had to solidify the bond before Michael found them and tried to come between them again.

"Come on, let's go." He grabbed her hand and pulled her behind him this time.

They were running then. Hand in hand. Running through the alley and out the other side. Running in the direction of the lake. It was late and there was nobody on the streets but even still they never paused or hesitated. Luckily the lake was on the same side of town as the Sherriff's office. They only had to make it through three streets and then they were outside of town, running together down an empty dirt road.

Zoey slowed and then slowed further and Rafe stopped as she struggled for air. Human. His brain reminded him and he winced at his stupidity. She couldn't run like he could. She didn't have shifter genes that gave her adrenaline and stamina. He cursed himself for not thinking about how far the cabin was when he'd simply started running.

"Baby?"

She dropped her hands to her knees and blew out a strangled breath, "I'm okay. I just... I need a second."

"No. You don't. You need a break." Rafe shook his head.

"No, I can go on. I can..."

He swept her up into his arms and marched into the woods just off the road. They were in the middle of nowhere. Had run at least a couple of miles. Nothing to him but well done for a human really. They were far enough out of town not to be spotted and she couldn't go any further.

It was time.

"Rafe?" Zoey glanced up at him questioningly, "What are you doing?"

"Claiming you."

Her breath caught and her eyes widened even as her pupils dilated, "Here? Now?"

"Do you want to wait?" He found a small break in the trees with thick grass and bent to lay her down.

Zoey bit her lip again, "No. I want you. I want to be yours."

He groaned as he kneeled down with her. Moonlight glinted off her coppery tresses. Her green eyes glittered against the background of the forest. She stretched and smiled up at him and he was lost. Completely lost in her and in them, in the mating bond and the future it would give him.

The heat lit his blood until he felt like he was burning alive. Sweat broke out all over his body despite the cool night. He'd heard about the mating heat. He'd heard that the longer a shifter put it off the worse it got but he couldn't imagine the heat getting any stronger than it was right now.

"Rafe, please..." Zoey shuddered when he reached back to pull off his shirt, "I can't wait any more."

Neither could he.

He dropped down and took her mouth. Claimed it. Just like he intended to claim her. It wasn't as sweet as that first kiss had been. They were too far gone for sweet now. It was all clashing tongues and teeth and moans.

He jerked at her clothes as they kissed. Fabric ripped. Her hands were all over him, stroking his chest and abs and anywhere else she could reach. Everywhere she touched burned hotter than silver. It was too much and not enough and his wolf was right there beneath the surface, growling for more of her, all of her.

He flexed his jaw and ground his teeth, mentally reminding his other half that teeth weren't allowed this time around. Not yet. He hadn't earned that from her. He hadn't earned this, earned her. Nothing he'd done so far in his life had warranted a gift like Zoey as his mate but he wouldn't screw this up. Not with her. She was the first bright spot in his life in so long.

Rafe pulled back enough to look at her and his wolf growled again. Naked in nothing but moonlight, all that pure, porcelain skin on display for him and him alone. She was a tiny little thing with soft curves and freckles he intended to trace with his tongue. But not tonight. Tonight, there would be no going that slow.

He cupped her breast with one hand and slid the other down to her slick folds. She was wet. Soaking wet. For him. And when he rubbed her she arched and moaned and wiggled beneath him, gasping his name and causing a jolt of awareness to slither in beneath the heat.

"Zoey..."

"Hmm?" She hummed, eyes closed, head tilted back with pleasure as he continued to tease her nipple and stroke her.

"Baby, look at me." He ordered firmly and her eyes slowly drifted open, glassy with a need that only made the answer to the question he had to ask that much more important, "You're not a wolf but you grew up in the pack. You know I won't judge you if you didn't wait. You're human. You couldn't have known you'd have a mate. But I... I need to know... if you... have you... will I..."

She softly reached up and cupped his cheek, stroking his hair back gently, comforting him when he found it difficult to ask the question. She must know what he was asking. Not just if she'd been with anyone, ever, but if she'd been with Michael. He didn't think so but the very thought, it unnerved him.

"I waited for you."

His heart clenched tight in his chest and his wolf eased back a little, pure pride in their little mate radiating from him. His wolf wanted to reward her for that. For saving herself for him and him alone. And the man was so overcome with emotions his throat felt tight.

She was his. His mate. And he would be her first, and last, everything.

"Mine. You'll only ever be mine."

"I always have been. It just took us a while to catch on."

Zoey smiled softly and leaned up to brush her lips across his, "Now claim me before I go out of my mind."

Bossy little mate. His nearly feral wolf grinned and Rafe did too. She was theirs. To protect. To cherish. To love. And all he had to do to keep her forever was seal the mating bond.

"It might hurt a little at first." He warned as he positioned himself at her entrance because he hated the thought of causing her pain.

"No. It won't. My body was made for yours."

Rafe's heart melted, crumbled, was simply putty in her hands. Fate had gotten it right. She was perfect for him. So sweet but smart and demanding and understanding as well. She was going to be the best mate for him and he would be the best for her too.

"Ready?" He groaned as her wetness coated his length.

"Since the moment I saw you."

He pushed in and her body welcomed him just as easily as she'd sworn it would. The perfect fit. She'd been designed to take him no matter his size or girth. Her body stretched to accept him and the hot, wet clutch of her made him see stars.

"Rafe!" She cried out as he plunged inside of her and he felt her nails claw his back and loved it.

Loved it even more as their bodies moved in unison. In and out, up and down, united in every movement. Loved it when he felt the heat swell between them and the sparks finally ignite. The mating bond stretched between them as their bodies joined. A string tied around his heart linked to hers as surely as the way their eyes connected as he made love to her there in the grass, in a meadow, under the moon and stars.

"Mine." He growled as his climax raced down his spine.

"I'm yours." She gasped as her body began to shudder.

"And I'm yours." He promised as he buried himself as deep inside of her as he could get and let loose the climax that he'd been waiting a lifetime for. The bond cemented in place, not just a string but an electric connection. Undeniable. They were well and truly mated now and nobody could keep them apart.

Zoey shuddered beneath him as her own orgasm took hold. She cried out his name. Screamed. Scratched him. And his wolf growled with approval. He wanted her to mark him as surely as he intended to mark her. When her climax finally ebbed, they collapsed together, naked, in the grass, breathing hard and sweaty and holding one another tight.

Rafe ran a hand through her tangled hair, loving the way it felt against his chest, against his chin. She fit him so well. For once, fate had given him a gift instead of a curse and he would cherish it forever.

"Mine." He felt Zoey's smile against his chest as she snuggled against him and yawned, "I like the sound of that."

CHAPTER 10

Rafe stared at her in wide-eyed wonder as she slept. Zoey. His mate. God, fate had such a sick and twisted sense of humor and yet... in the end, it always, always got it right.

Zoey. His Zoey. He had to resist the urge to reach out and touch her, to stroke her and hug her and keep her close. To protect her. It had been a long time since he'd given a thought to protecting anyone, even himself. But he would protect Zoey.

She was more than just his mate. She was his other half, the one person that could make him whole. She was his salvation.

The fire he'd built flickered over Zoey's beautiful face. Her hair glittered coppery in the firelight and he wondered if he would ever find the right name for the color, ever get tired of looking at it, feeling the soft strands slip through his fingers. Her skin was soft, creamy perfection and though her face didn't have a single flaw, a single freckle, he hadn't missed the trail of them over her shoulders and down her chest, wanted to kiss each one, trace them with his tongue, map every inch of her, because she was his.

After she'd fallen asleep in the woods, he'd carefully carried her the rest of the way to the cabin. He knew that it was more than just sleep keeping her sedated. What they'd done in the woods had been so much more than sex. They'd mated and that meant her body and mind were in the midst of some major changes. She was still human, for now, so he'd built the fire even though he wasn't chilly because he wouldn't let anything touch her, anything hurt her, not even a cold.

While she slept, he'd looked around the cabin and silently cursed his brother yet again. This cabin had been his. His and Gabe's. Not Michael's. But like everything else Rafe had left behind, it seemed his little brother had attempted to claim this too.

He grit his teeth until his jaw hurt as he noticed all the improvements. All the proof that this cabin had been used in his absence. Not just because he could scent his brother. Not just because it was fully furnished, if a tad bit dusty. But because his mate's scent had been here even before he brought her inside.

She'd come here with Michael and that grated on his already frayed nerves.

It made his head hurt. Made his subconscious ask questions he wasn't sure he would like the answers to. Because he wanted the best for Zoey, for his mate, and at every turn he seemed to run into proof Michael would have been the better choice for her.

Michael was the one who had stayed. He'd taken over the pack. He'd taken care of everyone. He had the history with Zoey. Decades of friendship and love and devotion.

He'd given her a place in the pack and a home. He was the one she'd turned to whenever she had problems and all of her best memories must have been with Michael.

Even in this cabin, there were hints of their time together. Fishing poles tucked in the corner, one of them with a pink lure. The cabinets were full of food he had a vague memory of her eating as a kid. Fruit Loops and Cheetos and other junk food Michael must have bought for her even though he didn't eat it. There were clothes tucked into the drawers of the chest in the bedroom. Tank tops and shorts and a tiny little string bikini that had made Rafe's wolf growl at the very thought of his mate wearing so little in front of another. She had things here, scattered all around, as if fate had been preparing this place to become her home.

Only, instead of him, it had been Michael coming here with her.

Rafe shook his head to clear the fog of jealousy that nearly overcame him. No. No. Fate hadn't gotten it wrong. Zoey was his. She was perfect for him. She was a link to his past, to his brother, perhaps to help him mend what he'd broken. She was his and if she deserved the best then that's just what he would have to become for her.

She deserved a good man, a good wolf, someone that put others first, had friends, and helped them when he could.

Now that he'd had her, mated her, sealed the first half of the bond, his mind was clearer than it had been since the moment he walked into Noir and scented her. He hadn't come back here for her. He hadn't known she was here. She had been a surprise.

He'd come back because he needed to talk to Michael but instead of talking, they'd gotten into an argument, then an all-out brawl. His brother had tranqued him and thrown him in a jail cell. His brother had tried to keep his mate from him and if it had been anyone else he would have ripped him to pieces. He certainly didn't want to talk to him now but a good man would, and he knew he would have to.

Rafe's friend was in trouble. He'd asked for help. Leo, an alpha in his own right, had asked Rafe for help and he knew that couldn't have been easy. Leo was the only friend who'd managed to keep track of him while he was running around feral and wild. He was a good man, a good wolf, and his pack was in trouble. He'd asked Rafe for the aid of the Moirae pack but that wasn't his to give. Not since he'd given Michael the position of Pack Alpha. But he couldn't just tell his only friend no either, so he would talk to Michael.

He figured it was only a matter of time until his brother tracked him down anyway.

Michael must know he'd escaped by now, and how. He would start by looking in all of the obvious places. Zoey's home. Her bakery, which Rafe had stumbled upon while searching her out earlier. He'd check the house and then the woods but he was a smart kid. He'd put it together and know where to find him. In the only place Rafe could still consider home. He was honestly surprised his brother wasn't beating down the door already.

He could only assume Michael or one of his wolves had found their spot in the woods, or would shortly. They'd scent him and Zoey. They'd scent what they'd done, scent the bond that had been forged, the magic of it. He'd thought that Michael might rush here in a fury over it but of course, that would have been Rafe's reaction, not his little brothers.

Michael was smart but calm and collected. He would know there was no use barging in tonight. That he couldn't stop it, stop them, anymore. That he'd failed. He would give them tonight, Rafe knew. He wouldn't interrupt. They'd be reprieved from his wrath until tomorrow.

Tomorrow. Which only brought the reality of his new situation to the front of his mind. Tomorrow was the full moon. He would shift tomorrow. His wolf would force him to now that he knew his mate needed claiming. And then there would be no holding him back. He would bite Zoey, mark her as his, and seal their fate forever.

He had no control over his wolf when he broke the skin. He hadn't since that day in the woods when the hunters had destroyed his world. He'd been scarred that day, physically and emotionally, but his wolf had been irreparably damaged.

If Rafe, the man, was half feral, then his wolf was that feral half of him. He was savage and uncontrollable. He saw nothing but threats, everywhere. He was scared and he was dangerous.

Never, not once, had Rafe shifted in the presence of another since that day. It was too risky. He couldn't put anyone else in danger like that. But he wouldn't leave Zoey, he couldn't. She was his mate. Even if he started running now and got as far away as he could, when the moon rose tomorrow night his wolf would head straight for her anyway and when he found her, he'd be in a state of panic, fearful of losing what he knew was his to take, and he'd ravage her if Rafe couldn't get him under control.

If he couldn't give him a reason to believe Zoey was already theirs.

Fuck, he cursed under his breath and scrubbed a hand over his face. It was too fast. It was all happening too fast.

He'd only just found her. The heat had forced them both into the human claiming as quickly as possible. But the wolf, the bite, he needed more time. He needed to give the wolf time with her, to learn to trust her, to earn her trust in return. He needed more time but they didn't have any.

Tomorrow was the full moon and he would shift. The only question was whether or not Zoey would shift with him. It would be safer if she did. If they'd already bonded and she had a wolf of her own to protect her from him if it came to that. But damn it, how could he ask her to give him that, give him everything she was, when he'd left once before already?

Damn it, he didn't know whether to cry or scream, to hug her close or to run in the other direction.

"Rafe?"

He jerked his head up at the sound of his name. Her voice was rough from sleep, raspy and sexy as hell. He'd wrapped her in a blanket but hadn't redressed her and she was naked under that quilt. His heart twisted in his chest. He thought anything and everything she ever did or said would be sexy to him. Not just because she was his mate but because she was her.

Zoey.

He'd been of age before he left Noir. He'd felt the pull towards her. He couldn't deny it, wouldn't, not anymore.

It had made him feel guilty. Lusting after his brother's girlfriend. Everyone had known, *known*, that Zoey and Michael would mate when they came of age.

So he'd tried to ignore the pull he felt towards her. He'd kept his distance from her, and from Michael when he could, because he couldn't wrap his head around how or why he was so fascinated by her. By her beauty. By her sense of humor. By her intelligence and wit. So when he'd been forced to interact with her he'd hidden it under derision.

She must've hated him back then.

He smiled at the thought of telling her about it now. Now, since she was looking at him with that soft, sleepy, look of affection. What he'd have given for her to look at him like that all those years ago. If she had, maybe he would have stayed. But she couldn't have known, just as he hadn't, that *this* was what awaited them.

"Rafe?" Her smile faded and her brows furrowed, "What's wrong?"

"Nothing." He caught her hand when she reached for him and pressed a kiss to each of her fingers. "Nothing at all."

Her lips flickered but she shook her head as she sat upright, holding the blanket over her chest, so they were face to face where he sat on the coffee table, "I wish I believed that."

Rafe was captivated by the electricity that jolted through him at her touch. He nuzzled her hand. Moved it so he could stroke her soft skin against his cheek. He wanted his stubble to leave a mark, to mark her in every way that he could. He wanted her scent all over him and his all over her. Rafe found her pulse at her wrist, felt it speed, and couldn't stop himself from licking over it, lapping at her and taking her scent inside of him.

"Rafe..." His name was almost a moan this time when she said it and he growled, low in his throat, because *that* was a sound he wanted to hear for the rest of his life. "Rafe, wait..."

He growled when she jerked her hand away from him and she giggled slightly. He met her gaze but despite the sound there wasn't humor there. She was watching him with those intelligent multi-colored eyes and he sighed, knowing that she wasn't going to let him ignore her question.

"What's wrong?" She tilted her head slightly and raised her hand of her own accord to stroke his cheek this time.

He shook his head and raised his palm to cover hers, to keep her touch there, "It's nothing."

"It's not nothing." She scooted closer to him, "I can feel it, Rafe. I can feel *you*. It's the bond. It's still forming, it's not complete, but I can feel you already, sense your emotions. Something is wrong and you're worried."

"Zo, I don't want to scare you. Let it be. For now..."

"No." She stated sharply and firmly, "You don't get to do that. You don't get to shut me out and claim it's for my own good. Not now." She cupped his face with both hands and forced him to meet her steady gaze, "You claimed me. You said I'm yours. You said you're mine. That means you have to talk to me. You have to tell me what's got you so scared."

Rafe winced, wanting to pull back. He wanted to run. He wanted to turn his back so she couldn't see it but that was the thing. She wasn't just seeing it. She could feel it. And no denying it would convince her even if he hated that word because he *was* scared.

"Rafe, please, you're not going to scare me away. I promise. Nothing can do that. I feel you, here." She moved one of her hands to take his and press it to her chest so he could feel her heart beating in time with his, syncing with his as the bond worked between them, "I'm not naïve enough to believe this is love. Not yet. But I care about you and I want you, all of you. You're already in my heart so don't break it. Tell me what's wrong."

He took a deep breath and let it out slowly. She was right of course. She deserved to know what she was getting herself into. She deserved to know everything, especially the parts that scared him because they were what would hurt her the worst. The bond was there but to seal it, she had to trust him and to do that, she had to know the truth.

"The bond isn't fully formed because I didn't bite you when we mated. I held back."

CHAPTER 11

Zoey flinched back as if he'd slapped her when his words landed. They stung and not just because they were a shock. They hurt because she could feel the bond stretching between them, feel the worry and fear that must have been simmering inside of Rafe. The heat, the intense longing, had settled some since they mated but now she could feel everything else he was feeling. Like remorse, and God did that hurt.

She hadn't wanted this. Just a few hours ago she hadn't wanted Rafe. She hadn't wanted a bond to him. Even when she'd felt the need to move towards him at the lodge she hadn't truly wanted to do it. But the heat had taken over, had made the decision for her and now it was too late.

He was a part of her. Inside of her. In her heart. She could feel him and it hurt... It hurt to think that now that the heat had waned *he* didn't want *her*.

He hadn't bit her. The words made her head spin. Made everything she thought she knew turn upside down. Because he hadn't bit her.

No. That wasn't right. He had. He must have. The heat

demanded they bond and it wouldn't be sated if they hadn't. But then the little voice in the back of her mind asked how much she really knew about the mating bond of werewolves.

She wasn't one of them even if she'd grown up around them. And bonds were intimate. Special. They were between the two mates. Not many talked about the magical experience so everything Zoey knew was going off of lore, small-talk and gossip really.

It didn't matter. She shook off the knowledge that she was in way over her head in this. Rafe had bit her. She knew he had. He'd said that she was his and he was hers. So he must have bit her...

But she raised her hand to her neck and found nothing but smooth, scarless, untouched skin.

Her memory of them in the woods played in a loop. The way he'd laid her down on the soft green grass. The way his eyes had blazed gold as he stripped her naked and followed her down. The heat of his kisses. The softness of his touch. The way he felt moving inside of her. The way her body had stretched to fit him as though it were made for him and him alone.

And yet, her eyes flashed back to his, "You..."

"Didn't bite you." Rafe confirmed softly.

She felt her bottom lip tremble, the rush of emotions from the half-formed bond was overwhelming. She couldn't discern her emotions from Rafe's. She felt so many different things all at once and she couldn't seem to hold any of it back. She felt tears well in her eyes and her vision blurred.

"Oh, baby, no... no. Please don't cry." Rafe was there instantly, his big, warm hands cupping her face, smoothing her hair back and swiping the lone tear that escaped from her cheek, "Please?"

His touch was soothing yet electric. It sent a surge of need through her but at the same time, it made her want to curl into his arms for comfort. She knew letting him touch her right now would only confuse her emotions more but she couldn't bring herself to pull away from him.

She wasn't strong enough.

"I.. I...I don't understand." She met his worried gaze and shook her head, "Why?"

"Why what?"

"Why?" She demanded more forcefully when he seemed confused, "Why didn't you bite me? You were supposed to and you didn't. Do you... do you not want me as your mate? Is it because of the Michael thing or..."

Zoey could feel the panic beginning to clog her throat. He didn't want her. He'd sated the heat but he didn't want a mate. He'd given in to it because there was no fighting the magic when it called but he didn't intend to seal it. Not fully.

This way, he could leave again. Leave Noir. Leave the pack. Leave her.

"Hey. Hey. Shhh." He cut her off, "No. It's none of that. No. Don't even think like that, Zoey. I want you more than I've ever wanted anything. You're mine. You're my mate."

"But..."

"But there are two parts to a claiming. My human half is yours, Zo. That's why you can feel my emotions. You must feel how much I want you. Right?"

She swallowed hard but managed a nod.

He was right. She could feel him. She was almost certain that it was the rush of his emotions that had woken her up. The conflicting feelings of what he wanted versus what he thought he could have. She could feel him and it felt... right.

Or at least it had until he told her he didn't bite her. He'd held back and mates weren't supposed to be able to hold back, not in the midst of a mating bond. It was magic and moonlight. It was strong. Stronger than any other force. But somehow, he'd resisted it and she didn't, couldn't, understand why.

"The second half of the bond is the wolf's claim." Rafe met her eyes, making sure she was with him, "It's a big deal to take a wolf's bite, Zoey and I didn't want to do it in the heat of the moment because there's no going back from it. Not for either of us."

"Is there any going back from... this?" She motioned between them, still confused.

Rafe sighed and released her to run a hand over his face, "If you wanted out..."

"I don't."

"Me either." His face softened fractionally, "The bond is there between us but it's only half formed until my other half claims you as well. I could've done it tonight, in the heat of the moment, but I wanted you to have a clear head and know what you're getting yourself into. I want you to *agree* to it instead of just having to accept it."

Zoey blinked but remained quiet instead of asking the dozens of questions on the tips of her tongue. Because Rafe was hurting. It was right there on his face but deeper than that, she could feel how worried he was. He had more to say and he didn't know how she would take it so she waited for him to find the words.

Rafe finally sighed again, "Do you know what happens when a werewolf bites a human, Zoey?"

"I... uh... a werewolf bite is lethal to a human nine times out of ten." She shook her head, "But not if the human is mated to the wolf."

"Right. If the human is mated, what happens?"

"Well, um..." She chewed her bottom lip and shrugged, "I become like you."

Rafe's eyes glowed gold with his wolf and he smirked, "Yeah, you become like me. That's the shorthand. You get a wolf, Zoey. Our bond will create a new wolf inside of you. You'll be dual natured. You'll change every full moon. You won't be human anymore."

Zoey was still confused, "I know all that, Rafe."

"Okay... well..." He dropped his head into his hands and didn't look at her, "What you don't know is that if the wolf doesn't do it right, it can be extremely dangerous."

"Dangerous?" She was about to ask what he was talking about again but he pushed to his feet and paced away.

Rafe was rubbing his face. Scratching his head. His shoulders were tense and everything inside of her told her that he was contemplating walking out the door. Walking away from her because of some perceived threat that she didn't even know about.

"Rafe!" She stood up too even though she felt a little dizzy when she did.

"Damn it, Zo." He spun to face her and was instantly at her side, guiding her back down onto the couch and tucking the blanket back around her, "Your body is still recovering from the mating. You need to rest."

"What I need is for you to tell me what's going on." She held onto him so he was forced to sit down beside her. "Why is finishing the bond dangerous, Rafe?"

"Because my wolf is dangerous." He admitted softly, "Michael was right. My wolf is feral. He's dangerous and I don't trust him with you. I'm afraid he'll hurt you."

Zoey softened, "Rafe, I'm your mate. You'd never hurt me."

"My wolf..."

"I'm his mate too."

"Not yet. Not until he bites you." Rafe pulled her into his lap and Zoey could feel how much he needed her touch, just as much as she needed his, so she cuddled against him and let him wrap her up tight, "Zo, in an ideal situation we'd have more time. More time for him to get to know you, to adjust to the idea of having his mate so close and to know that we finally found our home. But we don't have time."

She nuzzled under his chin, "Because the full moon is tomorrow?"

"Yeah." He was stroking her hair softly, "The full moon is tomorrow and I don't know if I can control him. He's liable to go crazy and attack you just to sink his teeth in you and claim you and I'm not sure he'll know when to stop."

Zoey's heart hurt with affection for this man. He was so scared that he would hurt her he was actually considering leaving her. Silly wolf. He wouldn't hurt her. She trusted him. Even if he didn't trust his wolf. Poor man. He was so broken but she could see it now, see that this was the first step in putting him back together.

"Rafe. He'll stop. He won't ravage me. I'm his mate."

He rubbed his cheek against hers, "You can't know that."

"I trust you." She tilted his face until they were eye to eye and she could see the worry in those fathomless depths, "I trust both of you."

"Zo..."

She kissed him. She didn't know how else to shut him up. And she wanted to kiss him. So she did. She pressed her lips to his and jolted at the spark of electricity that flared between them. The bond, it had to be. Attraction and lust and something deeper, something that she knew without a doubt would turn into a deep and unending love if they were open to it. She kissed him and he groaned slightly before taking control from her.

His lips devoured hers as if he'd been starving for another taste and she wrapped her arms around him. Dominant man. Her dominant man. Her mate. He kissed her just as passionately, as deeply, as he had when the heat was between them and she melted for him all over again. She was silently cursing the clothes he'd put on while she was sleeping when he nipped her lip and pulled away.

"Zo..." He groaned her name this time as if he was struggling. "I have an idea."

"Me too." She nipped his lips right back and he growled at her.

That sound. Oh, that sound was going to drive her crazy. It made her wet and needy and she wiggled in his lap until he securely held her still with his hands on her waist.

"Zoey, focus." He met her eyes but there was a mischievous glint there that she thought she might become addicted to very, very easily, "I have an idea but I need to ask you something first."

"Okay." She bit her lip and nodded as seriously as she could manage with heat running through her veins again.

"Do you want me to bite you and give you a wolf? You won't ever be rid of me if you do. I'll never leave you. I'll protect you from everything, including myself. I swear I'll be yours and only yours and I'll do my damndest to be the kind of man, and mate, that you deserve."

Zoey tangled her hands in his hair, "Rafe, you're already my mate. I trust fate. I trust you. And I trust your wolf. I told you, I'm yours."

The relief that washed through her was his. She was already getting better at picking out her emotions from his.

JESS BRYANT

She was made for this. For him. She'd trust him enough for the both of them until he learned he could trust himself again.

"If I bite you tonight, my wolf might be more controllable tomorrow. Maybe. I don't know for sure but... I think if I mark you then he'll understand that you're already ours and there's no need to hunt you down and *take* you."

She swallowed hard at the way he said it. His wolf hunting her down and ravaging her definitely didn't sound like a nice way to spend their first full moon together. She wanted his wolf to like her, want her and trust her. That wouldn't happen if he thought he had to *take* her, as Rafe put it.

"Then bite me." She smiled softly, "Mark me. Claim me, Rafe. I want it. I wanted it in the woods."

"Your head wasn't clear in the woods. I'm still not sure it's clear. The bond..."

"Is getting stronger, just like you said." She cut him off with a soft kiss, "I know you're scared but you don't have to be. Not anymore. You're not in this alone."

He tangled his hand in her hair, a low sound coming straight from his chest that made her wince because it was so sad. He'd been alone for so long. He'd lost his family and his mind and control of his wolf that day in the woods. He'd left Michael behind and he'd lost the pack and his position in the process. He'd been out there running wild, all alone, ever since. But now he had her and she wasn't going anywhere. He needed to understand that from the start.

Rafe pressed his forehead to hers, "The bite, it'll bind us together forever. No going back. You'll be a wolf and she'll be as mated to mine as I am to you."

Sweet, broken man, so worried about her that he was

still giving her ways out of this but she shook her head, "Bite me, Rafe."

"My wolf…"

"Mark me." She cut him off.

"It might not…"

"Claim me." She wrapped her arms around him and straddled his lap, "Claim me, Rafe. I'm your mate."

His eyes looked pained as she pushed away the blanket he'd wrapped her in even as a low growl worked in his chest, "Zoey…"

"I trust you." She met his eyes again, "Now, let me see him."

Rafe frowned but his wolf was already so close to the surface she felt the ripple of magic and power even before his eyes flashed wolf. The gold glowed and the growl in his chest went from sexy to dangerous in a split second. She didn't flinch, simply met those gold eyes and softly stroked her mate's cheek.

"I trust you." She told the wolf in her man's eyes, "Don't hurt me. Please."

Rafe squeezed his eyes shut and shook his head firmly, "Never."

CHAPTER 12

Zoey traced the scar that ran across Rafe's temple. It pinched when he winced like this. Otherwise it was almost invisible. She wondered if he'd gotten it during the attack on his family but she didn't dare ask. Not yet.

Someday. Someday they'd know everything there was to know about each other. Someday they'd have a foundation of friendship and love and support. They would have their someday because she wasn't going to back down from this.

Fate hadn't made a mistake. Maybe the heat had been driving her before. The need to touch and feel and secure the bond had been pulling them together from the moment Rafe walked back into her life. But her mind was clearer now and she knew, this, the two of them, mates, was right.

She pressed her lips to the scar and felt Rafe shudder beneath her. So she does it again, and again. His hands slide around her waist, his arms pulling tight so she kept going. Peppering kisses across his scar and down his cheekbone, along his jaw as he held her close and she could feel the swell of too many emotions to name. She pressed a soft, sweet, kiss to his lips and he kissed her back for a second before pulling away.

"Zo..."

"Shh..." She tried to kiss him again but he shook his head seriously.

"If we do this, there's no going back. We belong to each other. Now and always."

Her throat felt tight and she couldn't find the words. Not this time. So she simply nodded.

Rafe kissed her then, wrapping one hand in her hair the way he seemed to like and she absolutely loved. He tilted her head just so and then he claimed her mouth with a slow, burning kiss that branded her lips and her heart and soul.

Her lips parted on a sigh and he deepened the kiss with a stroke of his tongue. It was so different from their kisses before, when the heat had been on them. Those had been passion and need, fire threatening to burn them to ashes. But this was something else entirely. There was still passion, still need, but the fire had settled into a simmer, one she had a feeling would burn between them forever.

Now and always.

God, how was it possible she was falling in love with this man already? She couldn't. She shouldn't. It wasn't possible and yet. With the bond strengthening between them, she could feel what he was feeling, knew it mirrored her own and amplified it.

The poor, broken man that had lost so much and given up even more. The sweet, caring man that had insisted she accept the bite instead of simply taking what his wolf must already see as his. The tough, determined man that had tracked her down and fought his brother to claim her.

He was hers and she was falling in love with him.

Rafe's big hands went to her ass, pulling her tight against him and she moaned into his mouth. She could feel him through the fabric of his clothes. Hard and wanting. Wanting her. Again. She arched her hips to rub against him. She could feel her own wetness. She wanted him. Again. Rafe growled low in his chest and then he was moving and she broke the kiss to squeal as he stood up.

"Where are you going?"

"Bedroom." He nipped at her jaw as he carried her through the cabin. "Gonna do it right this time."

Zoey wrapped herself around him and nuzzled his neck. The words were on the tip of her tongue to tell him just how right it felt. Nothing had ever felt so good as being in his arms. Being wrapped up in his warmth and safety soothed the raw parts of her that had spent years alone, wondering why fate had been so cruel.

Now she knew. Fate wasn't cruel. It was twisted and convoluted. It was impossible to change and no matter how hard you fought, there was no denying it.

Rafe was her fate. He always had been. But he hadn't been ready for her when she came of age. He'd been half-crazed from his parents and brother's deaths and he'd been feral. If he was worried about claiming her now she knew he would have ravaged her then. So he'd gone away, for years, and they'd both been all alone, healing, trying to find their place, until finally, fate saw fit to bring him back home, back to her.

Finally.

Rafe carried her into the bedroom but surprised her when he didn't lay her down. Instead he sat on the edge of the bed, keeping her in his lap, and kissing her deeply.

His hands stroked over her ass now, kneading and pulling, shifting her on top of him so that his hard length hit her in all the right places. Only, he was still dressed and she couldn't have that. She unwound her arms and desperately searched for the hem of his shirt.

"Off." She broke the kiss as she tugged the material upwards and though he made a low noise of protest he raised his arms for her.

Zoey gasped when she got a good look at his chest. In the woods, she'd been drunk on the magic of the heat. She remembered him taking off his shirt so that they were skin to skin. She remembered stroking her hands all over him and feeling the raised marks. But she couldn't remember actually seeing the scars until now.

Puckered, round scars dotted his right side from chest to hip in a random, haphazard pattern. Bullet holes. The scars from when he'd been shot. She remembered that day. It had changed the entire pack. She'd known Rafe was shot but she hadn't seen him then and somehow, in her mind, no matter what she'd heard since, she hadn't imagined it was this bad.

There was no way he should have survived this. She traced her fingers over the scars slowly, carefully, and felt anger and sadness well up inside her. Someone had hurt her mate. Tried to kill him. And if they'd succeeded she never would have even known he was hers.

"Hey." Rafe's voice was rough as he tipped her chin up to meet his gaze, "It's okay. I'm okay. I'm here. With you."

Her throat felt tight again but she nodded. She could feel him tense when she touched the wounds. Knew she should leave them alone. She should focus on making him feel good, on sharing this night with him and sealing their bond. But she couldn't do that without showing him that she understood the importance of these scars, of what he'd lost, and of what she represented to him.

A future.

Zoey leaned down and kissed the first scar lightly. It was just below his collarbone. Rafe made an inhuman sound that she recognized as his wolf's pain, like at the river, and she steeled herself for him to push her away. Instead, his grip on her tightened. She continued, kissing down his chest, replacing the pain of the scars with what she hoped was comfort. When she got low enough that she couldn't comfortably bend any further she slid off his lap to kneel at his feet on the floor.

"Zoey." Rafe growled and when she glanced up she saw the gold of his wolf in his eyes.

"Let me." She whispered, ignoring the warning in his eyes as she kissed another scar and moved her hands to work open his jeans.

Rafe was panting now. Petting and stroking her hair. But he still didn't push her away when she ripped open his button and unzipped him. His cock sprang free as she pushed the material aside and her core clenched with need.

He was big, but of course he was. She knew that already. He was superhuman after all. Part man and part beast. And she'd been made for him, her body had taken him, welcomed him, and wanted him again so badly she could feel the wetness on the inside of her thighs.

But first, she wrapped her hand around the thick base of his shaft and basked in the sound he made. Half growl half groan. She stroked him slowly, root to tip, and when a bead of moisture gathered at the fat head she couldn't resist leaning forward and lapping it up with her tongue.

Rafe cursed and his hands went to her hair, fisting so

tight it stung, but it only made her pulse pound and her clit throb. She licked him again, and again, and he let her so she sucked him into her mouth and took him as deep as she dared. Another round of cursing and then his hips were bucking beneath her, driving his length into her mouth while his hands held her head still to take him.

It was bliss. Pleasure. Untold ecstasy. To know that she could make this strong, powerful man come apart. Lose control. Want her this much. She had to clench her thighs together to keep from coming as he groaned her name like a prayer.

She knew the female shifters in the pack didn't like this act. They talked about it. Freely. Their wolves considered it subjugation to be put on their knees. Even the submissive wolves only did so once they'd established their position with their mate.

But Zoey loved it. Loved this. Loved that Rafe lost control when she touched him like this. Loved the taste of him, the sounds he made. And she also knew by the end of the night she would be getting a wolf of her own so this might be her only chance before her wolf tried to assert dominance and refused to kneel.

Rafe's hips stuttered and Zoey clutched at his hips. He was close. She could feel it through the connection. He was desperately trying to regain control though and she knew before he pulled out of her mouth that he wasn't about to let the night end before it even got started.

With a growl, he hauled her up and then tossed her onto the mattress. He loomed over her before she settled. He pinned her arms above her head, notched himself between her thighs and kissed the living hell out of her.

Zoey moaned and tried to pull him closer. She needed

closer. Needed more of his skin on hers. Needed his scent all over her. In her. She needed him to come in her again. Wanted to feel him deep inside her. But no matter how she wiggled and bounced she couldn't get him where she wanted him and it only made her more desperate.

Apparently, she liked controlling alpha males. Which was good. Because that's exactly what she'd gotten.

Rafe broke the kiss with a groan, "I can taste myself on your tongue. Me and you. Intertwined. It's fucking perfection."

He kissed her again and her eyes rolled back into her head. He sucked on her tongue and she whimpered. He teased and played, swirling and swiping and owning her mouth until they were both long overdue for breath and they broke apart panting.

"Fuck, love the way we taste." He groaned as he trailed kisses down her neck and nipped at her ear, "Maybe I'll eat you up after I come inside you. Taste you there once you're full of me. Would you like that?"

The words pouring out of his mouth were filthy and sexy as hell. Zoey moaned and whimpered. She was incoherent with need now, just like in the woods. Only this time there was no blaming the heat, it was just the two of them. They were this good together.

"Rafe, please..." She begged as she struggled to free her arms.

"What do you want, baby? Tell me and I'll give you the world."

"You. I want you. All of you." She panted as he shifted his weight, holding her down with one hand as the other slipped between her thighs to tease her, "Do it. Please. Make me yours."

"You already are." He growled and she watched

through slitted eyes as he sucked on the fingers he'd been teasing her with, "This is mine."

"Yes."

His eyes flashed gold and his nails elongated and when he growled, it was almost pure wolf, with Rafe's voice just beneath, "Don't want to hurt you."

"You won't."

He was positioned to take her. She could feel him at her entrance. And when he paused, those gold eyes on her, she could see his teeth too were longer. He wasn't going to shift but his wolf was there, with them this time. And he wanted to bite her.

"Do it." She insisted desperately, "Your wolf needs his mate and I need to belong somewhere."

"You do belong. With me. You're mine." He all but snarled as he drove inside her and she screamed his name in pleasure as her body pulsed around him.

Heaven. This man was hers. Being with him was a gift. She didn't know if it would always be like this between them. If it was the heat waning or the full moon rising or if it was just the bond, that they were mates. But she had never felt like this before, like she was right where she was supposed to be.

"Rafe!" She cried out as he plunged in and out of her, fast and then faster still. "So close, so close, so... Now. Do it now."

Her climax hit her like a lightning bolt and a moment later she felt the sharp plunge of teeth in her neck. She screamed at the mix of pleasure and pain. She was electrified, everything inside of her felt as if she'd suddenly grabbed hold of a live wire.

Somewhere in the haze, she could hear Rafe say her name. Hear him tell her to hold onto him. That it was all going to be okay. But as the pleasure of her climax ebbed and the full brunt of the bite took control, she realized there was a reason nobody in the pack ever talked about the mating bite.

It was because it wasn't heaven but pure and absolute hell.

CHAPTER 13

I t felt like fire was burning through her blood. Somewhere deep inside of her, it felt as if something was being ripped apart. Her soul maybe, but that didn't make sense. The claiming was supposed to bind the two mates together not rip one of them to pieces. It felt like claws digging into her heart, shredding it until nothing was left but the pain.

It hurt. Oh God it hurt. She felt tears well in her eyes and she tried to scream but there wasn't any air in her lungs. No air. Just fire and heat, scraping at her throat until she was sure flames would erupt from her mouth.

"Rafe!" She squeaked out, panting and convulsing, her vision blurry with tears. She was dying. She knew it. She was dying just when she'd found her other half, her reason for being. She had to tell him, had to, couldn't leave him like this. He'd blame himself just like he had for the others. "I... I... don't..."

"Shh. I'm here." He cut her off with a soothing tone that did nothing to stem her panic because he was holding her down. Her arms were pinned above her. Her legs trapped underneath him. She was trapped and burning alive in her own skin. "I'm here. Hold onto me, Zo. It's almost over."

Over? What was almost over? Her life? Had they been wrong? A werewolf bite killed one in ten humans. If she wasn't truly Rafe's mate it would kill her. It had killed her.

She was crying. Screaming. Writhing beneath him but he wasn't panicking at all. Her mind tripped over that fact. Why wasn't he panicking? Couldn't he feel her fear through the bond? Couldn't he sense that she was weakening? That she was dying? It was almost over.

"I... I..." She tried to tell him... But then it happened.

It was as if an explosion had gone off. She was sucked out of the bubble she'd been trapped in. The one full of heat and fire and pain and death. She was dropped back into full consciousness, back into her body, and as she sucked in a gasp of sweet, glorious air for the first time in far too long, she gasped.

She wasn't alone anymore in her body. She could feel it. Sense it. Her wolf. She had a wolf inside of her. She was there, pacing just beneath the surface. Shaky on her newborn legs but strong.

"Oh, God..." Zoey choked out on a sob of hysteria.

"Shh, it's okay. You're okay." Rafe came back into focus and at the sound of his voice her wolf rubbed up against her skin, wanting to get to him, to touch him, and she practically purred when he stroked her hair, softly petting her, "You're okay now. You're more than okay. You're perfect. Both of you."

Her wolf rubbed at her insides again and Zoey tried to remember to breathe. All of the times she'd thought about bonding about mating and she'd never, not once, given a thought to what it would feel like to share her body with an animal. A wolf that lived inside of her. That was part of her but also separate. A wolf with her own wants and needs and desires. Her wolf wanted closer to Rafe and since Zoey couldn't really blame her she snuggled in closer to him and let him pull her against him.

She had no idea how much time had passed. How long did it take to birth a new wolf into existence? She and Rafe were both still naked, still locked together on the bed. Both breathing hard and trying to get their bearings. But she could feel his pride simmering through the current between them and it made her wolf preen with his approval.

"She's beautiful." Rafe murmured against her hair, "Just like you."

Zoey rolled to face him, eyes wide, "Can you read my mind now?"

He chuckled and she stared at him in awe. He'd laughed. Rafe Hudson had just laughed for the first time in God only knew how long and it was because of her. She'd put that look of pleasure and contentedness on his handsome face. She'd made that rusty, ill-used sound come from his chest.

And her heart slipped a little further out of her grasp when he smirked at her with that mischievous, dimpled smile, "Kinda."

"What do you mean, kinda?"

He chuckled again, "I mean, the bond is even stronger now so I can sense your mood and emotions. I can tell just from the vibes you're sending out if you're happy or sad or..."

"Angry that you're reading my mind?" She sniffed but he surprised her by laughing again and then rolling her over until he had her pinned again. "Hey!"

"I'll know when you want to fight and I'll know when you're just looking for a way to provoke me." He nipped her lips and settled between her legs again, "I'll know exactly what my little wolf needs and when she needs it."

Zoey moaned and her new wolf all but purred, Wh... What does she need?"

"What she needs..." Rafe nipped at her lips before kissing her softly, "Is to rest. She's strong. I can feel how strong she is. But she's still a newborn and you both need time to rest and recover from the change."

"That's not what she needs." Zoey argued when her wolf lunged for him.

"It's exactly what she needs." Rafe argued with another kiss, "Even if what she wants is to meet her mate. It's not happening. Not tonight."

"But..."

"Not tonight, Zo. You've already talked me into too much. The mating and the bite and the bond." He rolled off of her but pulled her into his arms, "I told you I would always give you what you need and right now, what you need is to rest."

She chewed her bottom lip and contemplated what he was saying. Her wolf didn't like it. Didn't like being told what she needed. Especially when it conflicted with what she wanted. But a yawn caught up to her and she supposed that Rafe was right.

It had been a long night. So much had happened. So much had changed. She'd thought she was dying just minutes ago. She had an animal living inside of her now. She was werewolf.

Finally, a small smile spread across her lips.

"We'll change together? Tomorrow?"

"Tomorrow." Rafe sighed heavily and she could feel the worry begin to seep in again as he thought of all the things that could go wrong when he let his wolf loose, "When the full moon rises, you'll shift for the first time and I'll... I'll shift with you."

The way he hesitated didn't give her a burst of confidence but she fought away the doubt, "Does your wolf... Can he sense her already?"

Rafe stroked his fingers up and down her spine. A caress for her. A pet for her wolf. She shivered and snuggled even closer to him, loving the strength and comfort of being in his arms.

"Oh yeah, he can sense her. He can see her. He's the one that told me she's beautiful. He wants her so bad my skin itches with the need to shift. But I'm keeping him under control, Zo. I promise."

"He's not going to hurt me, Rafe."

"I know." He said, but there was no conviction in his tone or in the bond.

She sighed and laced her fingers together with his, "Tonight, we'll rest but tomorrow you have to tell me how all of it works, okay? I may be pack but I wasn't one of you. Not really. Not until now."

"I'll tell you everything you need to know."

Her wolf harrumphed and circled slowly before laying down. She wasn't giving up. Like Zoey, she was stubborn, and like Zoey, she didn't miss that Rafe's words weren't what she needed to hear. He hadn't promised to tell her everything. Only what he thought she needed to know. It was a start but it was by no means the open and honest relationship she needed from him.

She attempted to lighten the mood, "We'll shift and we'll run and we'll play in the woods tomorrow night then? Like hide and seek?"

Rafe snorted with amusement, "Kinda. We'll shift and

run together only, when my wolf catches yours, he's going to mate her Zoey."

Her eyebrows rose, "He's going to... they're going to... in wolf form?"

"Mmhmm." He sounded amused again. "How did you think they sealed their bond? The same way we sealed ours. When they mate, the circle will finally be complete and our bond will be cemented in every way and in every form."

"Oh..." She really hadn't given that much thought either but she didn't think now was a good time to point out that whenever she'd thought of mating a wolf in the past she'd thought of Michael and her living happily ever after, not exactly the schematics of how it all worked. "Will I... we... know what's going on?"

"Yes. You'll still be in control of your wolf. She has her own spirit but she lives inside you. She's a part of you. There's no way to separate one of you from the other now. So just like you can feel her there in the back of your mind like this, when you're in wolf form, when she's the one at the forefront, you'll be in the background, able to whisper to her and guide her."

Zoey relaxed against him as she contemplated his words. She would still be the one in control. But Rafe wouldn't be in control of his. He'd told her as much earlier, before she'd agreed to the bite. He'd lost control of his wolf that day in the woods when the hunters attacked and he'd never regained it. She couldn't help but wonder how it must feel to him, to be pushed to the back of his own mind when his wolf took over, unable to control what the animal did.

"He won't hurt you." Rafe's voice was rough when he spoke and she silently cursed the connection she'd forgotten about for a second there. He didn't know exactly what she was thinking. But her change in mood must have been enough to give away her train of thought.

"You sound a little more convinced than you did earlier at least." She squeezed his hand.

Rafe sighed heavily and raised their joined hands to kiss her fingers, "He's... content. I can't remember the last time I could've said that but he is. Being here with you, like this, your scent on me, mine on you, it calms him."

She kissed his chest, just over his heart, "That's a good sign, right?"

"I think... marking you tonight was a good idea. It settled some of his nervousness. He knows you're ours now and he can sense your wolf. He can feel how strong she is, knows he has to be strong for her too. She's a good mate for him."

Zoey smiled softly, "Fate huh?"

"Sometimes she gets it right." Rafe stroked her hair softly.

A twinge of something she couldn't quite place ached in her chest. Fate got it right. So why did she feel that flash of irritation, or remorse and sadness? It wasn't hers, she realized when it began to soften at the edges while Rafe combed her hair.

She was picking up Rafe's emotions again and she had a pretty good idea what had triggered that one this time.

"I didn't mean it like that." She murmured softly.

"Hmm?"

"Don't play dumb. You know what I'm talking about. Down at the river, everything was happening so fast and I was in shock. Rafe, I didn't mean it when I said fate chose the wrong wolf for me."

He stopped stroking her hair, "Yes... you did."

"Rafe.."

"But it's okay." He tilted her head back until he could look her in the eyes, "It's okay. You were in shock, like you said. You have a history with him. Our bond, our mating, doesn't wipe away the years you two spent together. I understand why you wish it had been him."

Zoey's heart was breaking at the resignation in his tone, "I don't. Not anymore. Not now that we're bonded and I..."

"It's okay." He cut her off with a soft kiss to the fore-head, "I thought it myself you know? That he would have been a better pick. He's the safe choice. Stable. Solid. But I can be those things for you too, Zo. I can be better for you. I promise."

She nodded instantly, tears welling in her eyes again, "We're good together. I know we are. And we'll be strong together, for each other, okay? We'll figure it all out but just know... I don't wish it was him with me here now. Okay?"

Rafe nodded and hugged her close. She wasn't certain how reassuring her words really were. They both knew it was the bond and the mating that had changed her feelings. The heat had driven them into each other's arms and now they were locked together forever. Whatever came next, whatever tomorrow brought, they would deal with it together.

"Zo..."

She nuzzled Rafe's chest when she heard him whisper her name and realized she'd been dozing slightly. Just on the verge of sleep. But he'd pulled her back, just barely, just enough to respond.

"Hmm?"

"I'm glad it was you."

She fell asleep with a smile on her face and her new wolf content because she was wrapped protectively in the arms of their mate.

CHAPTER 14

R afe watched her sleep for a long time before finally convincing himself and his wolf that losing sight of her wouldn't mean losing her. She belonged to them now. Just as they belonged to her. So despite his overwhelming need to keep her close, to protect her, he kissed her softly on the forehead and then crawled out of bed.

He wasn't sure how much he'd slept. Not much if the aches and pains were anything to go by. The heat and then his desire for Zoey had managed to conceal the worst of it last night. But in the light of day, his back was sore where he'd been shot by the tranquilizer and he felt groggy as if the drugs were still in his system.

As a shifter, he had enhanced healing abilities. He should have been fine by now. He could only assume that since Michael had upgraded the local jail to hold shifters that he'd also upgraded the weaponry his officers carried. There was little doubt in his mind that tranq had been specifically designed to take down a shifter if he was still feeling the effects hours later.

Typically, the first thing he did when he woke up was go for a run. It helped to work off some of his innate shifter energy. He didn't let his wolf out enough and it made them both restless. A good solid couple of miles in the morning worked off the worst of the agitation but he couldn't bring himself to leave the cabin.

Not with Zoey still sound asleep in the other room.

He didn't want her to wake up alone. That's what the reasonable side of his brain told him. The reasonable side of him said that she'd been through a lot last night. He'd flipped her entire world upside down. Hell, he'd literally turned her into a different species. The least he could do was be there for her when she woke up.

But the reasonable side of him also knew that wasn't the full truth.

He couldn't get too far away from her because if he did, she might get hurt. She might get attacked. She might wander off and get lost. She might leave him and she couldn't leave him. Not when he'd just found her. Not when he'd finally found his mate. Found his way home. He couldn't lose her, not like he'd lost Gabe and his parents. So he didn't dare leave the cabin, instead choosing to shower and dress and then make breakfast for his little mate for when she woke.

Besides, he told himself. He wasn't being overprotective. Trouble was going to come for them sooner rather than later. They'd had the night together. A gift, really. But it wouldn't be long now until the forces that had tried to keep them apart showed up to check the damage done.

Michael was coming. It was only a matter of time. And Rafe intended to put himself between his brother and his mate this time. Because she was his and there was no way Michael was taking her from him.

Rafe scrambled the eggs in the frying pan much harder than necessary as he thought about that. She'd said last night that she wasn't disappointed fate had given her him instead of Michael but how could she not be? He was a mess compared to his brother. He didn't even have control of his wolf. But he'd heard the truth in her statement when she said she didn't wish it was Michael with her now. She'd said it and she'd meant it. He could only hope that she still did today, in the bright light of morning, without the heat baring down on them or the power of the mark compelling the bond.

He was just plating the eggs and pulling the bacon off the griddle when he heard the door to the bedroom open. He steeled himself with a deep breath, but all it did was force more of her sweet scent into his lungs. He turned to face her and the simple ease of her smile caused an uncontrollable pain in his chest.

God she was gorgeous.

Fresh from sleep, her hair tied up into a messy ponytail and her face free of makeup she looked even younger than she was. More like the girl he remembered. She'd found some clothes in the dresser, a disappointment since he was a big fan of her naked. Luckily though, the tank top and shorts she'd donned didn't cover much and he could still see and stroke plenty of her smooth skin. Then his eyes caught on the mark on her neck and his wolf practically howled with approval.

She hadn't covered it up. In fact, pulling her hair up showed it off. The loose tank top cut low exposing the spot where her neck and shoulder met, right where he'd bitten her.

The wound had healed overnight but she would bear his mark for a lifetime. The semi-circle imprint of his teeth in her flesh glistened silver-white in the morning light. And just like that, he was hard and his teeth ached to bite her all over again. Everywhere. So no matter what she wore, everyone would know she belonged to him.

"Good morning." She grinned as she moved towards her.

His eyebrows twitched upward, "Is it?"

"Of course it is." Zoey pranced over to him and didn't stop until her body was right up against his, she tiptoed up and brushed her lips over his as she wound her arms around his neck, "Would have been better if you were still in bed with me though."

He groaned as her soft body brushed his and her taste ignited his system. Sweet, sexy little mate. He could feel desire pulsing off of her as clearly as he could feel his own. She wanted him again. Still. And he could only hope always.

Rafe forgot all about breakfast and feasted on her mouth instead. He cupped her ass and dragged her up his body. Zoey wound her legs around his waist and moaned into his mouth. Two steps and he had her on the counter-top, a second after that he had his hand down the front of her shorts and they both groaned.

Wet. She was so fucking wet for him. Already. Wanted him. Needed him.

"Rafe." Zoey tilted her head back and arched her hips up into his touch as he stroked through her folds.

"Love it when you say my name like that." He groaned against her neck as he kissed her everywhere he could reach. She'd showered before coming out of the bedroom and she didn't smell like him anymore. That was something he had to fix. Now. "Say it again and I'll let you come."

"Rafe!" She cried out as he found her entrance and

plunged a finger deep, pulled it out and inserted a second, curling them until he found the spot that made her shake and moan, "Rafe, please."

"Anything you want. Always. You just tell me and it's yours." He rotated his fingers until he could get a third inside her and pumped them in and out while he thumbed her swollen clit, "Tell me, baby."

"Make me come. Please, Rafe, make me come." Zoey gasped out hoarsely and then screamed his name as he pinched her clit and she fell over the edge into her orgasm, "Rafe!"

She screamed his name so loud he was certain the other wolves could hear her in town and damn if that didn't fill him with a sense of pride. He wanted them to know she was his. Wanted the world to know that he was the one that could give her this pleasure.

Zoey collapsed against him as the tide ebbed, "Oh my God..."

"Mmm, good morning." He smirked as he pulled his fingers from her panties and raised them to his lips. She watched, glassy eyes wide, as he licked them clean. Her eyes riveted on his mouth he felt another surge through their connection, knew exactly what she was thinking, "You want another good morning kiss, baby?"

Zoey bit her lip, feigning shyness, as her cheeks turned a pretty shade of pink but she nodded and damn if that wasn't his undoing. She was his. His mate. Perfect for him in every way. Rafe took her mouth again boldly, swiping his tongue deep so she could taste herself on him just as he'd tasted her last night. She moaned and kissed him back until the buzzer on the oven went off and he reluctantly had to pull away.

"Wha..."

He kissed the end of her adorably confused nose, "Hold that thought, babe. The biscuits are burning."

She eyed him as he turned and pulled on an oven mitt and then pulled a pan of fresh baked biscuits out and put them on the counter to cool, "You cooked breakfast?"

"Yeah."

"You know how to cook?"

He snorted, "Of course I know how to cook. I've been on my own for years. What'd you think? I was out there running wild chasing down rabbits and squirrels for dinner?"

She rolled her eyes, "No. I just... I don't know. Never mind. Forget it. The food smells fantastic."

"Thank you." He moved back between her legs since she hadn't moved from the counter and offered her a piece of bacon, "I figured you'd wake up hungry. Just didn't know if it would be for me or for food."

"Maybe a little bit of both." She grinned at him as she took a bite of the bacon he offered and then closed her eyes and moaned.

The situation in his pants became nearly unbearable when she made that sound, "That good huh?"

Her lashes fluttered open, "Not as good as the orgasm but close."

"Close huh?" He chuckled at her teasing and pushed the plate of bacon aside, "Guess I'll just have to do better this time."

"Mmm, sausage too huh? I'm such a lucky girl."

He barked out a laugh at her sass, "What you're gonna get is bent over that counter and fucked, little mate."

Her eyes glittered as if he'd made it a dare, "Do your worst, big bad wolf."

"Never." Rafe wrapped a hand in her luscious copper

colored locks and pulled her mouth to within an inch of his, "You only ever get my best."

He took her mouth again and she wrapped her arms around his neck. God, he could get used to this. Waking up next to her. Teasing and playing. Fucking her senseless. She wasn't the lucky one. He was.

She reached down to unbutton his jeans at the same time there was a loud slamming of a car door. Zoey jerked backwards so hard she slammed her head into the cabinets. She cursed and Rafe growled at the intrusion. He cupped her head softly and she winced when he touched the knot that was already beginning to form.

"You okay?"

"Fan-freaking-tastic." She whined.

"It's not cut. Just a bump. It'll heal quickly."

"Says the werewolf with enhanced genetics."

He raised an eyebrow, "Zo, babe, maybe you hit your head harder than I thought. You do remember what we did last night right?"

She rolled her eyes at him again, "How could I forget? You put a wolf in me." She wagged her brows and then frowned and rubbed her head, "It was just a reflex."

He understood then as she sat rubbing her bruised skull. She'd been human all her life but since the age of ten she'd lived amongst shifters. Whenever they got hurt, they shook it off because bruises healed in minutes and breaks in mere hours. She'd probably had a hundred skinned knees and busted lips and she'd had to wait for her human body to heal her while everyone around her went on with their lives like nothing had ever happened.

His poor little mate had been hurt and he hadn't been there to protect her.

This time the intruder pounded on the door and Rafe

barely contained a vicious growl. He wanted to ignore it. Wanted to go back to his nice morning with his mate. Wanted more orgasms and bacon and eggs. But he knew there was no putting this off and honestly, he didn't want to.

He wanted Michael to see them like this. Wanted him to scent what they'd done last night. See what they'd just been doing. He wanted his brother to understand that their scents were mixed now, that they were mated, and that there was no use fighting. He wanted Michael to go away and leave them alone for the next twenty-four hours to twenty years but since that wasn't a possibility he would take this.

Zoey frowned, "Who the hell is at the door?"

Rafe frowned right back at her, "You don't know?"

"I mean. I can guess." She sighed heavily and her shoulders sagged.

"You can guess?" He tilted his head confusedly, "You mean, your wolf doesn't sense him?"

She shrugged and shook her head. Rafe scratched his jaw. That was weird. Zoey was a member of the Moirae pack. She had been since she was a kid, human or not. Her wolf, even newborn, was automatically a part of the Moirae pack, which meant she should have been able to sense her Pack Alpha.

Unless... Rafe scowled at the idea. Unless Michael wasn't her Pack Alpha. Unless he'd somehow created his own pack with her since he was a born Alpha too.

The banging on the door came again and this time Michael growled through it, "Open the damn door. I know you're in there. I scented you from a mile away."

Rafe almost smiled at that. Almost. He liked that his brother had caught their scents already. Michael knew what it meant. Zoey was his. He also liked the idea that if

Michael had been close enough to scent them earlier that he'd probably also heard Zoey coming from Rafe's touch.

Maybe that made him an asshole. He didn't much care. He wanted, and needed, as much evidence as he could get that Zoey belonged with him so Michael couldn't take her away.

But he didn't smile because Zoey pushed him back and jumped off the counter, landing on her feet and straightening her clothes, "I'll talk to him."

"Like hell you will." Rafe growled.

"He's my best friend."

"And he's my brother, so what?" Rafe scoffed, "You're not going out there."

The banging on the door came again, "So help me Rafe, don't make me knock this door down. Get your ass out here. Now!"

Zoey started to step around him but Rafe caught her by the arm, "Stay."

"I'm not a dog." She growled at him and he could sense her wolf it was so close to the surface and angry.

Rafe softened his stance and cupped her cheeks, "I know you're not a dog, Zoey. You're a wolf. My wolf. My mate. You're mine to protect so you're going to stay inside and let me deal with Michael."

"The only one that needs protecting from Michael is you."

"Please just stay here. I need to talk to my brother and I can't do that if I'm worrying about you getting in the middle of us."

"I wouldn't..."

"Please?"

Zoey sighed and nodded, noticeably unhappy about it though. He kissed her forehead when she huffed at him but since her wolf wasn't showing through anymore he decided it was safe to step away from her.

His own wolf was pacing under his skin. He didn't like the idea of another male being anywhere near his mate. Not right now. Not when the bond wasn't solid and that wouldn't happen until the wolf got his chance with her tonight during the full moon.

Rafe opened the door and found his brother standing on the other side looking pissed off and more than a little disheveled. Michael's eyes flashed gold at the sight of him and Rafe let his own wolf flash back at him. If Michael had come looking for a fight, Rafe would give him one.

He hadn't fought for the pack or for his right to stay but he would fight for Zoey, for his mate, even with the only brother he had left.

CHAPTER 15

"**M**ichael." He stepped outside rather than inviting his brother in.

"Rafe."

He raised an eyebrow when his brother refused to step back and give him room. Tension swelled in the small space between them. Two born Alphas going head to head and refusing to be the one to give first. As the younger, it should have been Michael that blinked but Rafe had given the pack to his brother. This was his land. Besides, Rafe knew Zoey wouldn't like it much if they came to blows so he did something he'd never thought he would do.

He lowered his eyes first.

Michael stepped back and he glanced up quickly enough to catch the look of shock that flashed on his brother's face before he masked it. Michael studied him momentarily and then he too looked away. Two Alphas that couldn't look each other in the eyes. Two brothers that couldn't find the words to mend all that had been broken.

Rafe cleared his throat, "Why don't we have a seat and talk?"

He motioned to the patio set on the other end of the porch. The one he figured Michael had bought and put out here. For him and Zoey. Rafe stepped past his brother, giving him his back to show he wasn't scared of an attack. For all that Michael had given Zoey, this was what Rafe could start with.

Michael didn't say a word, simply stomped over and dropped himself into one of the chairs.

Rafe glared at the man standing a hundred yards from the house between two cars. On the left was a silver Jeep. On the right, a jacked-up truck. The man glared right back at Rafe and crossed his arms over his chest.

He dropped into the chair nearest the door, "Was the Enforcer really necessary?"

Michael shot a look over his shoulder and shrugged, "He drove my truck out for me so I'd have a ride back. I drove Zo's Jeep. I thought she'd want it so she could get back to town."

"She's not going anywhere." Rafe growled a warning.

Michael only leaned back in his chair and scrubbed a hand over his face, "I didn't mean today. Just... whenever." He shifted again, clearly uncomfortable, "I'm not stupid. Far from it. I know it's too late to stop you. I just have one question for you now."

"Okay."

"Are you staying?"

Rafe flinched at the question, "What?"

"Are you staying? Here. In Noir. Are you coming home to the pack? Because she's pack. She's family. She's *my* family. And whatever life you've been living out there on your own, you can't drag her away from the only home and family that she has."

Rafe stared at his brother for a long moment, trying to

figure out where they'd gone so wrong. It was his fault. He knew. He had left without any explanation. He'd stayed gone because he'd thought it was for the best. Not just for him but for Michael too. Now that he was back, now that he had Zoey to think of, he knew just how badly he'd screwed up.

He'd left his brother behind. He'd been so messed up about losing his family that he hadn't given much thought to the family he had left. Michael. He'd left behind a scared teenage boy to run a pack all by himself after burying his parents and older brother.

What the hell had he been thinking? The truth was. He hadn't. His wolf had been crazed and feral. He'd been in shock and grief. And he'd run. He'd run away thinking it would solve his problems but it had only created more.

It had created this rift between him and his brother that he wasn't sure anything could bridge, but he had to try. Not just for Zoey's sake. For his and for Michael's too.

Rafe dropped his head into his hands and his wolf whined, "I'm so sorry, Michael."

Nothing but silence greeted his apology. He'd expected that. In the face of everything, all the years and time he'd stayed away, it wasn't much. Not nearly enough.

"I'm sorry I left. I'm sorry I left you behind. I was... so messed up. I wasn't thinking straight. Hell, I still don't think straight most days. My wolf is feral. Practically uncontrollable. But I always thought when I got my shit back together I'd come home. I just... I never got it together."

He glanced up and saw that Michael's jaw was twitching. He was grinding his teeth together. He was also staring off into space instead of looking at Rafe and he felt the refusal to even acknowledge him like a punch in the gut. Even if he deserved it.

"So," Michael finally gritted out, "You came back for a reason. You said on the phone there was an issue I needed to know about. What was it?"

"Michael..."

"No." His brother snapped his eyes back to him and they glowed gold again, "No. We're not talking about her. Not yet. Right now, you tell me why you came back to *my* pack, to *my* land, to talk to *me*. You didn't come back for her so you don't get to talk to me about her. Not yet."

Rafe's wolf bristled at every word. He wanted to bare his teeth. He wanted to remind Michael that he was the elder, that he was the rightful Pack Alpha. But he didn't. Because he didn't want to be Pack Alpha. Had never wanted it. Michael was better at it than he ever could have been and the proof was right there in his statement.

Michael loved Zoey, in one way or another he always had. He'd called her his family. But before dealing with her, Michael had to know what the threat to the pack as a whole was, the one Rafe had come home to talk to him about.

Pack first, that was Michael. Rafe was the selfish one. He'd thought only of himself when he left. Now he had Zoey and he was thinking only of the two of them. Of keeping her for himself. But he had to talk to Michael first, put things right, or as right as they could ever be between them at this point.

"It's Leo. He's in trouble. He asked me to get the Moirae pack involved but that's not my place. I told him the best I could do is talk to you."

Michael's lips set into a thin line, "Leo DeLuca?"

Rafe nodded.

"He's Crescent pack, right?"

"Yeah. He said he'd have come to you himself but he's afraid it'll only cause more trouble for his family if he's seen meeting with you. Their new Pack Alpha is bad news and Leo thinks once he's done tearing their pack apart, he'll come for the Moirae pack. Something about you providing refuge for the wolves that have left the Crescent."

"I knew there was something going on in the Crescent pack. We've been getting a lot of transfers from there in the past couple of months. I've asked why but they all say the same thing, disagreements with new leadership." Michael scrubbed his jaw again, "It's a new guy. Maddox something. I've been meaning to check it out but the diplomacy of it all is... tricky. I can't just walk onto their land and accuse their Pack Alpha of something no matter what I think he's doing."

"What do you think he's doing?"

"Abusing his power."

Rafe nodded when he realized he and his brother were on the same page, "Leo fled or he swears he'd be dead right now. The guy challenged Leo's dad when he was ill knowing he couldn't take him at full strength. Killed the Alpha, killed his wife and took Leo's siblings as hostages."

Michael gaped at him, "Hostages? For what? What's he asking for?"

"He wants Leo dead too. He's the last male in his line. The DeLuca lineage would die with Leo and the Alpha can set up his own as a new dynasty. He says he'll let the younger sisters go if Leo gives himself up..."

"But?"

"But..." Rafe nodded when his brother caught onto where he was going, "He won't let the oldest sister go. He wants her for himself. Leo says he always has. He thinks she was part of his grab for power all along. That claiming her would unite the pack behind him even after the terrible things he's done."

Michael's scowl darkened, "And she's not his mate?"

"According to Leo, no."

He watched his brother scrub his jaw again and the familiarity of the act warmed some hollow piece of his heart. Their father had done that a lot when he was thinking. Michael reminded him of their father right now. Thinking. Plotting. Refusing to act until he'd put all the pieces together. It drove Rafe crazy. If he'd been in charge, he'd have swept into the Crescent pack the moment Leo came to him, seized control and then sorted out wrong from right.

Michael shook his head, "So, what's he want from us? To challenge this new Alpha on his behalf? To sneak in and steal back his family members?"

"No. He only asked that when he returns to challenge the Alpha that we have his back."

"He doesn't think the bastard will fight fair." Michael nodded, "I don't blame him considering he challenged the previous Pack Alpha during an illness. He's holding hostages and he intends to claim a wolf that isn't his mate. Those are some pretty serious allegations."

"I know. That's why I came to you. I'm standing with Leo. I came home to ask if you'll stand with me."

Michael eyed him for a long moment, openly assessing and then snorted, "That's why you came home after all this time?"

"Leo's a loyal friend, a good man and a good wolf. He's earned my help but I'm no good to him in a fight. I can't unleash my wolf like that. I don't trust him not to attack at random."

"But you trust him with Zoey?" Michael scoffed.

Rafe winced at the blow he should have seen coming. He'd known it was coming and he still hadn't been prepared. Because Michael had refused to talk about her until now. Now, when he could throw it in Rafe's face that he wasn't good enough for her.

"She's my mate, Michael." He said evenly. "*My* mate."

"Yeah, well she's my best friend and I'm the one that's been there for her so..."

His wolf growled, "Don't. Don't try to excuse what you did. You tried to keep her from me. Mate trumps best friend. Mate trumps everything. She's mine and you had no right to come between us."

"I had every right!" Michael raised his voice, "You said yourself you don't trust your wolf and I don't trust you with her!"

"That's because you love her." Rafe shook his head sadly.

Michael flinched, "Yes." He scrubbed his jaw again when Rafe growled. "But not like that. Not like a... mate should. She's my best friend. I want the best for her."

"It's more than that, Michael. Don't try to deny it. We're still family. I can sense how you feel about the girl."

Michael was the one that dropped his eyes this time, "I wanted her to be mine so badly. All those years together, we were so sure it was the two of us and then it was like, everything changed. I was Pack Alpha and you were gone and when she turned eighteen... she wasn't mine. I didn't handle it well. I know that. But I never expected for it to be *you* and I handled that even worse."

"Yeah, you did." Rafe nodded.

"You just, you walked back into town yesterday and turned everything upside down. I was scared. Scared of losing her. Scared of losing the pack. Scared of losing you again too." Michael met his eyes and this time there was no wolf, no anger, just the sadness and the distance that seemed to be a gulf between them, "I don't want you to leave again, even if it means giving up the pack."

Rafe blinked in confusion and then shook his head, "Jesus, Michael, no. I don't want the pack. I never did. I didn't come back for it and I'm not staying for it. I'm staying for her. She's all I want. She's all I've ever wanted. A chance at a home and a life, at regaining a piece of myself I thought I lost forever... my family."

"You never should've left."

"I know." He winced at the accusation in his little brother's voice.

Not the voice of the Pack Alpha. Not the voice of the man that he'd become in the years since Rafe left Noir. Just the voice and the accusation of the scared kid he'd been when his older brother abandoned him to all of this responsibility.

"If you'd stayed, maybe it wouldn't all be so fucked up. I would've given up on the idea of her being mine a long time ago. I would've had to accept it instead of keeping her around like some kind of consolation prize and hurting both of us in the process."

"Zoey is no man's consolation prize, Michael. You should know that better than anyone. She's the best. She's everything I could ever want or need in a mate. She balances me and she soothes my wolf and I swear to you, just like I swore to her, I'm going to be the best I can be for her because she makes me stronger."

"You better." Michael flickered a sad smile, "Or I'll snap your neck."

CHAPTER 16

Zoey was totally eavesdropping. Not that she was doing it on purpose... or at least she hadn't started eavesdropping on purpose. It was a wolf thing. Her hearing was far superior to what it had been just yesterday. She wasn't standing with her ear to the door or anything. She didn't have to. She was still standing in the kitchen, chomping on a piece of bacon, which was surprisingly delicious and cooked exactly how she liked it. But she'd heard every word that Rafe and Michael said.

At first, the tension she'd felt coming from her mate had worried her. She'd worried the two of them would come to blows again. The tone Michael had taken with him bristled her wolf and made her frown. When her friend had snapped at Rafe, she'd almost stormed out onto the porch and gotten between them. Which was exactly why Rafe had told her to stay inside.

He didn't want to put her in the middle. He knew she cared about Michael. Just like he knew Michael cared about her, loved her even. But mostly she thought that he'd been worried if she got between them it would be to take Michael's side. It was a silly, insecure thought and she hated that she'd put it in his head. Because yesterday it might have been true but today it was impossibly inconceivable to her.

She cared for Michael. She always would. He was her best friend and she loved him. But what he'd said about not loving her like a mate should... she finally, finally, understood that. Because that's how she felt too.

Her attraction to him was gone and with her head and her heart a little clearer she could accept that a lot of what she'd wanted with Michael was to belong. To be one of them. Her parents were loving and supportive. The community was inclusive and welcoming. But she wasn't a wolf and she'd always felt like an outsider here... except when she was with Michael.

He'd been her first friend and she'd clung to him fiercely. She'd made him the center of her universe. Just like he'd clung to her when his parents died and his brother left town. Even when they'd learned they weren't mates, they'd clung to each other for reassurance that it would all be okay.

It hurt a little to hear Michael call her a consolation prize. She couldn't deny that. But she also couldn't deny that knowing what she knew now, he would have been hers too.

Because Michael didn't need her. He never had. He was strong enough to stand on his own. But Rafe wasn't. Rafe needed her in a way that she *needed* to be needed.

Listening to the two brothers talk, to try and set things right, she saw now just how right fate was to pair her with Rafe. Not just because the attraction between them was off the charts. But because she was the bridge that could span the distance between him and Michael.

She wasn't the one that would divide them like she'd feared last night. It was done. She and Rafe were mated. Michael couldn't change that and he'd seen the error of his ways. The only thing they could do now was move forward.

She was the reason they were talking, fixing things, and she knew just how badly Michael had always wanted Rafe to come home. Like she knew from the bond, from Rafe's swell of emotions, that he wanted to mend what he'd broken between them. They were brothers and despite all of their differences, despite all the years of absence, she could feel the love between them.

It warmed her heart.

What didn't warm her heart, was the way Rafe talked about himself. As if he wasn't good enough for her. As if he needed to be better. He'd said something along those lines last night but she'd thought he just meant healing his wolf. Listening to him talk to Michael she realized it went deeper than that.

"I'm not going to hurt her." Rafe swore. "She's my mate. I'd die before I let anything hurt her."

"But you can't control your wolf. You said as much." Michael countered.

Zoey huffed as they continued arguing and her own wolf stretched and shook inside of her. She didn't like Michael's tone any more than Zoey did and she'd had enough. They were talking about *her* now. She'd stayed out of it while they discussed pack business but this was her life too. She got a say. Final say even.

"He controlled his wolf perfectly fine with me last night." She strolled onto the porch as casual as could be and plopped herself down into Rafe's lap.

She grinned at him when his eyebrows winged up. She

could feel his surprise through the bond. He hadn't expected her to come outside? Really? She pressed a quick kiss to his lips. No, that wasn't it. He hadn't expected her to stick up for him.

Silly wolf. He was hers. She'd always protect him. Even from spats with his brother and his own inner demons.

"I..." He groaned slightly as she settled more firmly on his lap, wrapping his arms around her automatically, "I thought I told you to stay inside?"

"Told?" She raised a skeptical eyebrow. "I think you asked."

He gave her a pointed look, "Yeah. Asked. That's what I meant."

She giggled slightly and nuzzled his cheek, "I did stay inside but I got lonely and I needed to touch you."

Rafe groaned again as she rubbed her body against his and she hid a smile in his neck. He was trying to stay strong. He wanted to send her back inside. She could feel it. But a bigger part of him was loving the way she touched him, kissed him, claimed him in front of his brother and for the world to see.

Good.

Because she had a feeling this whole wanting to be around him constantly, wanting his hands on her body, his skin against hers, wasn't going to go away anytime soon. So Michael might as well get used to it. Now.

Rafe was hers and she was free to touch him and kiss him wherever and whenever she damn well pleased. Her wolf practically purred when he pulled her closer. She kissed him again, a little harder this time and nipped at his lip with her teeth before pulling back and glancing across the table as if she'd just remembered they had company.

"Michael." She smiled sweetly, "Nice of you to visit."

His eyes were wide with a look of shock that made her want to smack him. He stared at her as if he'd never seen her before and she glared back at him. He shook his head and squeezed his eyes shut as his jaw all but hit the table.

"Holy shit, you're..."

"Amazing?" She shrugged, "I know."

He snapped his jaw shut and glared at her as color creased his cheeks, "I was going to say, a wolf." He growled and his gaze darted from her to Rafe and then to her neck where the mark was clearly visible, "You're a fucking wolf! What the hell, Rafe? You turned her!"

Rafe tensed as the air sparked with magic and fury but he didn't get a chance to respond. Michael was on his feet in an instant and his eyes flashed gold. Zoey was slung into the air and tucked against Rafe's back as he stood just as quickly.

"Don't." He growled at his brother.

"Michael..." She tried to step around Rafe to calm the situation that had spiraled out of control but he only snagged her and tucked her safely to his side.

Her best friend shook his head again, "Jesus, Zo. You let him bite you? One fucking night together and you let him bite you!"

Her own wolf snarled at the disgust in Michael's tone. He was angry and she didn't understand why. But it pissed her off.

"Oh, no. No, no, no." She pointed a finger at him, "You do not get to judge me for bonding with my mate."

"There's a difference in bonding and taking a bite, Zoey." Michael threw his hands in the air, "Fuckin' hell, he can't control his wolf. He's feral! And you let him bite you! He could have just as easily ripped your throat out!"

"But he didn't." Zoey forced herself not to yell at her

best friend. "He controlled himself. He controlled his wolf. I'm his mate. He would never hurt me. You know that. Despite whatever else you might think, you know that."

"You don't even know him." Michael sighed.

Rafe growled but Zoey touched a hand to his chest and he stilled. This wasn't his fight. This was hers. Because she knew where Michael was coming from now. He was worried about her. Trying to protect her. It was all he'd ever done. He was just going about it all wrong.

"So, you're going to what? Slut shame me? You're mad I accepted the bond and the bite so easily? No. You don't get to be mad about that, Michael. I'm not yours. I was never yours. But you know damn well that if I had been, we would have sealed the bond the day I turned eighteen, no questions asked and no looking back so you can take your judgmental bullshit and stick it up your ass."

Michael opened his mouth, closed it again and then dropped his head into his hands with a curse. The sparks that had filled the air between them all began to fizzle and she felt Rafe settle next to her. She kept herself tucked to his side and rubbed his back reassuringly. Michael dropped back down into his chair with a heavy sigh and she knew that she'd finally gotten through to him.

"I'm not judging you."

"Sure sounded like it."

"I'm just... worried." Michael looked up and his eyes were back to their normal hazel color.

She met his familiar gaze with a firm nod, "I know. You worry about me. It's what you do. But I'm not yours to worry about anymore."

"That's the thing..." Michael looked from her to Rafe and then back to her again, "You're not mine."

"I think we established that last night." She groaned.

"No." Michael shook his head, "You don't get it. I was shocked because I couldn't feel your wolf. I didn't sense her until you came outside and revealed yourself. You're not mine, Zo... and neither is she."

"Son of a..." Rafe cursed under his breath.

She could feel whatever ease her touch had given him evaporate. He tensed and almost stopped breathing. She could hear him audibly swallow hard.

"What? What's that mean?" She glanced between the brothers who both looked confused and more than a little freaked out. "What does that mean, Michael? Rafe? One of you tell me what's going on."

"Your wolf." Michael scrubbed a hand over his face in his universal tell of frustration, "She's not mine, Zo. She's not Moirae pack. If she was, I'd have felt her the moment she was born. I would have sensed her."

Zoey blinked in confusion, "What do you mean sensed her? You said you sensed her when I came outside."

"My wolf senses her the same way we can sense any supernatural being but you're not his. She's not his." Michael frowned and looked at his brother, "What the hell did you do? She's not part of my pack anymore. How did you give her a wolf that's not pack, Rafe?"

Zoey let the words sink in and turned to her mate with a wary expression. He looked as shocked and confused by Michael's words as she did. She wasn't pack. She had a wolf but she wasn't Moirae pack. It didn't make any sense. This was her home. Michael was her Alpha. Human or wolf, she was Moirae pack.

"Rafe?" She questioned softly when he cursed again.

"I don't know." He answered her unasked question, "I don't know. It... I..." He growled and tugged at his hair, "I mean, it explains why you couldn't sense it was him at the door. If he was your Alpha then your wolf should have sensed him. I..." He swung a panicked gaze to his brother, "Are you sure?"

Michael glanced at her warily, "Yeah. I'm sure."

The two men stared at one another for a long time and Zoey felt her breathing speed. She could feel Rafe's unease. His panic. Something was wrong and they weren't telling her what it was. She wasn't pack. Somehow, she was a wolf and she still didn't belong.

"One of you tell me what that means. Now!" Her voice rose with her own panic.

"Hey. It's okay. Shh. It's okay." Rafe pulled her into his arms and she only realized when she was enfolded in his safe embrace that she was trembling, "You're mine. It just means that you're mine."

"I don't understand." She bit her lip and nervously glanced at Michael for reassurance.

Her friend was standing up again, hands on his hips, "It means what he said. You're his. So is your wolf. He's not just your mate. He's your Pack Alpha."

"What?" She tore her gaze back to Rafe and saw the answer in his eyes. "You're my Alpha? We're not... Moirae pack? How is that even possible?"

Rafe was Moirae pack. He was a born Alpha of the Moirae pack. She'd been adopted into the Moirae pack. How could the two of them together created a wolf that wasn't?

Michael finally spoke up with a sad expression, "He broke ties with the pack and he stayed gone too long. His wolf doesn't recognize the pack as home anymore. He's feral. Wild. Unbound to any land or anything, until you." Michael scrubbed his face again, "Your bond anchored him and since he's an Alpha, it means you two started your own pack last night."

"Michael." Rafe's voice was rough with emotion, "You have to know I didn't intend for this to happen."

"I know." Michael snorted, "You didn't intend for any of this to happen but fate has her own ideas about where we should be and who we should be with."

"Michael..." Rafe tried again but his brother cut him off with a cruel laugh.

"I guess it means you were telling the truth at least. You didn't come home to take the pack from me. You really don't want to be part of the Moirae pack at all."

Zoey could sense the hurt in Michael's words and from the way Rafe tensed she knew he could too. Rafe had come home. Michael had gotten his brother back. But Rafe had lost his link to the pack and now he'd taken Zoey from them too.

"Michael..." She reached out for him but he stepped back and she winced at the slice of pain his avoidance caused. "Don't. Don't be upset. It just... happened. He didn't plan it. We didn't even know!"

"I know." Michael nodded again but he wouldn't look at them, "It explains a lot though. Explains why our wolves are so at odds. Two Pack Alphas on the same land. Two Pack Alphas fighting over a member of their pack. Mine wanted to keep Zoey human so she was Moirae. Yours had to make her a wolf to create yours. Two Alphas this close to one another, with a claim on one person, of course it caused trouble. Alphas of separate packs aren't meant to coexist peacefully."

Zoey frowned at that. What did that mean? The pack dealt with plenty of other Alphas. Michael met with all the local packs once a month to keep the peace. How was this different?

"This doesn't have to mean what you think it means." Rafe frowned. "We're not leaving, Michael. We're not starting our own pack. I may be a born Alpha but I'm not Pack Alpha material. Not anymore. I claimed Zoey. She's mine. Fine. But as far as I'm concerned, our pack is big enough with just the two of us. We're not going anywhere."

Zoey could hear the truth in everything that Rafe said. She could feel the worry that he was losing his brother again, right in front of his eyes. They hadn't known. How could they have known? But Moirae pack or not, she knew Michael well enough to know that he was upset and that he didn't quite believe his brother.

He didn't trust him. Not yet. Not after he'd left. Not after he'd stayed gone for years. Not when he didn't trust Rafe with her.

She bit her lip, "Babe, why don't you give me and Michael a minute to talk?"

Rafe growled low in his throat.

"Stop it." She turned to face him and forced him to look at her, "You're asking him to trust you, right? Trust that you're not taking me away from my home and my family? Trust that you didn't come here to break up the pack?" Rafe gave a slight nod. "Then I'm asking you to trust me. Let me talk to him. Alone. Please?"

"Zo..."

"I know." She reached up and cupped his face, "I know you're worried about me but you don't have to protect me from Michael. He's your brother and he's my best friend. He won't hurt me."

"Never." Michael confirmed from behind her.

Rafe growled again but he gave another nod, "Fine. I don't like it, but fine."

"Thank you."

"The Enforcer stays with me though." Rafe snapped over her head. "He stays here where I can keep an eye on him and you stay on the property, where I can sense you and get to you fast if I need to. That's the only way this happens."

Zoey rolled her eyes, "Rafe..."

"Deal." Michael spoke over her and then, louder, "Darius, I know you heard all that. Get your ass up here and keep my brother company while Zo and I go for a little walk."

Rafe glared, "Where I can see you. At. All. Times."

Zoey sighed, "Okay but..."

"No buts." Rafe swept down and sealed his lips over hers, stopping her protest before it could even get started.

If she'd been teaching Michael a lesson when she'd kissed him earlier, Rafe was giving him a show.

He took her mouth as if he would never get to taste her again. Heat flared despite their audience and she moaned and tiptoed up for more. He took advantage and swiped his tongue into her mouth, greedily stroking hers until the fire between them threatened to burn out of control. She whimpered when he broke the kiss just as quickly as he'd started it and he smirked as if he was proud of himself.

She smacked his chest playfully, "Possessive bastard."

He caught her hand and kissed her palm before placing it over his heart, with a shake of his head "Possessive mate."

"Yeah, yeah, we all get it." Michael snorted from behind her, "You already marked her no need to tattoo your name on her forehead. She's yours."

Zoey blushed slightly but that only made Rafe's grin

widen even more. God, he actually liked the idea of tattooing his name on her. She rolled her eyes and pushed away from him despite her hormones itching to climb him like a tree.

"I'll be right back." She promised.

"I'll be waiting." He swore right back and then glared at his brother, "And watching."

CHAPTER 17

I t was strange, being so close to Michael and not feeling anything but the warmth of familiarity. No longing. No sadness. Just comfort and friendship.

Still, she'd ducked inside and pulled a jacket on over her tank top. She'd thought it would make Rafe a little more accepting of her talking to his brother privately. Instead, he'd unzipped it and pulled it to the side, kissing her mark that he'd put back on display before letting her step off the porch.

Darius glared at her as she slipped past him and she contemplated flipping him off. Asshole Enforcer. Darius was stone cold and he cared about exactly one person and one person only. Michael. He protected his Pack Alpha at all costs and he'd clearly decided that Michael now needed to be protected from her.

She didn't bother waiting to comment on it until they had walked out of earshot because they were all wolves here now, "I take it Darius now considers me the enemy?"

Michael shot a look at his Enforcer and his friend, "Don't take it personally."

"Oh, I'm taking it personally because that's exactly what it is."

"Zo," Michael used that warning tone with her, "He protects me from anyone that's not pack."

"And I'm not pack anymore." She scoffed, "So it doesn't matter that I'm your best friend? That I'm your brothers mate? I'm a threat now?"

"No. You're just... different. And Darius doesn't like different. He doesn't like change."

"Yeah, neither do you."

Michael scrubbed his face and then tucked his hands into his pockets, "You're right. I don't. I don't like surprises and I don't like change and I really, really don't like that you're a wolf, Zoey."

She winced, "You really never wanted me to be a wolf, did you?"

"No."

The slash of pain in her chest surprised her. She hadn't thought her heart would still hurt so badly to know that Michael had never considered her worthy of truly being part of his pack. Somehow, her wolf growling at him didn't surprise her at all though. She was strong, even newborn, and she wasn't a big fan of Michael saying she shouldn't exist.

He sighed, "It's not what you think, Zo. It's just... being what I am, it's controlled my entire life. I never had a chance to make my own decisions. Being a shifter, having a wolf, it takes away your freedom and I never wanted that for you. I wanted so much more for you than this life."

Zoey jammed her hands in the pockets of her jacket and considered what he was saying as they walked along the edge of the forest. She knew Michael wanted the best for her. She'd always known that. But she still couldn't understand why he thought there was a better life for her than this one.

The one fate had chosen for her.

"Michael." She chose her words carefully, "This is the life I've always wanted. To be one of you. To be a wolf and truly be part of the pack. To be with..."

"Me." He snorted, "You wanted to be with me."

She winced because she'd been going to say that she wanted to be someone's mate. She wanted that kind of love and devotion. The kind that meant two souls were stitched together as one. But he was right too, as much as it made things awkward. She wasn't confused anymore. She didn't want Michael anymore. She only wanted her mate because he'd given her those other things.

"Michael..."

"Don't bother denying it, Zo. I know you. I know you wanted it to be me just as much as I wanted it to be you."

She groaned because she knew those words would hurt her mate, could practically feel him flinch through the bond, "But it's not. It's not and we were only hurting each other pretending otherwise. You said so yourself."

"I know."

"So why can't you just be happy for me?"

Michael sighed, "Zo, if I thought you were happy maybe I could be but..."

"I am." She growled when he shot her a skeptical gaze, "I am!"

"Zo..."

"Damn it Michael! You're a wolf. You can sense that our scents are already mixing. You can sense our bond and it's strong. I know you damn well heard us before you slammed that car door and..."

"That's the heat." He growled.

"No. It's not." Zoey stopped walking and shook her head at him sadly, "The heats waned. It pushed us together but it's not what's keeping me here. I'm here because this is where I'm supposed to be. This is where I want to be. He's who I want to be with. He's who I was *meant* to be with."

She meant every word. Rafe was hers. She was his. Their wolves would bond tonight and the circle would be complete, just the way fate intended it. Whatever thoughts she may have had about fighting it when she first found out, whatever confusion she'd felt when she spontaneously developed feelings for Rafe that outweighed years of what she felt for Michael, she knew there was no going back. And she didn't want to.

She finally belonged and it was with Rafe.

"You don't know what you're getting yourself into." Michael argued.

"Look, I know you're still trying to protect me but..."

"No. It's my turn to say something." He turned her around by the shoulders until she was facing the cabin, until she could see Rafe standing on the edge of the porch watching them. His shoulders were tense and his eyes were narrowed and she could see him scowling even from here, probably because Michael was touching her. Michael continued, "You think his bossy, protective stance is what... hot right now? It's hot that he wants you this much. But it'll get old, Zo. You can't stand being micromanaged and he's going to try and control your every move."

She pulled away from Michael's hands, "He's my mate. Of course he's going to be protective."

"It's more than that. After what happened to our parents, to Gabe... he's never going to be comfortable letting you out of his sight."

Zoey's heart squeezed at the reminder of all her mate

had lost, of all her friend had lost, and just why it was so important for them to find a way to come back together, if not as pack, then as family, "I know he's had a rough time but I think... I think that's part of the reason fate put us together. For this. To bring him home and keep him here. To help you two fix things."

"You can't fix him, Zo."

She turned back to face her friend, "I can try."

"He's feral. His wolf is uncontrollable."

Her jaw clenched, "He controlled his wolf last night. He's in control with me. The bond, it helps."

Michael's throat bobbed and she knew he was swallowing something he wanted to say. Something that would likely piss her off. She knew him well but he knew her too. This wasn't a fight he could win. It was already done. It was time to move on... for both of them.

He finally sighed, "Just don't get your hopes up, okay?"

She narrowed her eyes at that, wanting to tell him, again, that Rafe would never hurt her. Instead, she did the same thing he'd done. She swallowed back the argument. Instead, she turned and started walking again and only once she felt him fall into step beside her did she try to lighten the mood.

"I think what you're meaning to say is, '*wow, look at that, I was right all along. You're my sister now and I'm so happy that you and my brother are going to build a life here in Noir where we can all be together.*' Right?"

Michael barked a laugh and Zoey smiled. That was a laugh she'd heard all her laugh. Michael had always been quick to it, at least with her. He was serious with the rest of the pack, with the rest of the world, but he was just Michael with her. Maybe because somewhere deep inside they'd always known they were family. Rafe's laugh sounded a lot like Michael's only rougher, like it had never been used. But maybe she could change that too.

They walked in silence for a bit before she brought up the real problem at hand, "We're not going anywhere."

Michael groaned, "Zo..."

"He meant what he said." She cut him off quickly, "He doesn't want to run away with me. He wants to finally come home. This is his home."

"Zo, two Alphas on the same land, even if he wants to stay... it's a bad idea."

"You really think your wolves will have that much of a problem sharing space?"

"Well they certainly didn't like the idea of sharing *you*, did they?"

She snorted, "It's different now. Rafe and I are mated."

"It is different now." Michael conceded, "You're not pack anymore." He must have seen her wince because he sighed, "I'm not saying that to hurt you. It's just the truth. You're Rafe's now. You belong with him. Fine. But neither of you are Moirae pack."

"Hey." She grabbed his arm and pulled him to a stop, "I'm Moirae pack. I'll always be Moirae pack. And Rafe's your brother. So is he."

"But..."

"You heard him. We're not starting our own pack. He never wanted to be Pack Alpha. If he did, he'd have stayed instead of giving it to you and leaving. He'd have fought for it when he came back. He doesn't want to be Alpha of a pack."

"It doesn't matter what he wants, Zo. He's a born Alpha. He has his mate. When you two make pups... they'll be part of your pack. Their mates and their kids will be your pack. They won't be Moirae."

Zoey almost smiled at the mention of her and Rafe having pups. She liked that idea. She liked it a lot. She really liked it that Michael was acknowledging she was Rafe's and that they would have a family together. But then it hit her in the gut that he was right. If she and Rafe weren't Moirae pack then their children wouldn't be either. And that hurt because she'd always wanted her children to be part of the pack that was her family.

Only, Rafe was her family now.

"And it doesn't help that the cabin is on Moirae land." Michael was still talking and she shook off the moment of melancholy.

Rafe was her family. They would make their own family. But her parents were Moirae pack. She would always be Moirae pack in her heart no matter what.

"What?" She blinked in confusion. "What's the cabin have to do with anything?"

"My wolf considers it his because it sits on his land. Maybe Rafe was supposed to be Moirae Alpha but he isn't. I am. It's mine. My wolf's claim on it still stands because the pack owns it."

"Property law? We're going to get into property law now?" She rolled her eyes, "That's an easy fix, Michael. Sell us the cabin and the land here around it."

"My wolf..."

"Won't like giving up part of what he considers his land. Fine. But isn't it better than driving me and Rafe away because your animal is a possessive bastard?"

Michael opened his mouth, shut it again and then sighed, "I'll think about it."

"Thank you." She nodded gratefully.

She hadn't expected him to simply agree. Giving up land was a big deal to shifters. Their animals bonded to the land. It was their safe place to run and be themselves in any form. Michael was a good Alpha and no good Alpha would give up his land easily. But she trusted that he would, because he wanted his brother to stay, wanted her to stay, even if he wouldn't say so.

They headed back towards the house and Zoey easily changed the subject by asking about the problem with the Crescent pack. Michael scowled at her and told her to stay out of it, that it wasn't anything he couldn't handle. Which meant he was intending to get the Moirae pack involved, and that made her smile.

He really was a good Pack Alpha. He couldn't stand the thought of a bad one destroying a pack. And, it had the added advantage that it was Rafe's friend that had asked them to get involved. They would stand together on this and then, when the time came, Michael's wolf would know that Rafe, and his pack, no matter how big or small they ended up being, would have his back.

Win. Win. Well, for everyone but that bastard Alpha, Maddox.

Michael stopped at his truck, "Stay safe tonight."

Zoey smiled, "I'll be fine. I promise. I'm going to change tonight for the first time, with Rafe, and we're going to finalize the bond."

"I know just..."

"He won't hurt me."

"I hope you're right."

Zoey hugged her friend for worrying about her. Michael wrapped his arms around her and hugged her tight. She smiled against his chest. Friendship. Family. That's all there was between them. All there had ever been, really, despite what they'd wanted. And that was okay, because this was what felt right.

"I'm not going to hurt him either." She said softly and Michael's grip on her tightened before he released her.

"Take care of each other." Michael smiled softly as he stepped back from her and motioned for Darius to come as he waved goodbye to his brother, "Please."

"Always."

Michael chuckled, "And don't let his wolf push you around too much."

"It's like you don't know me at all." She winked as she slid past a still glaring Darius and back towards her mate.

He was scowling. Of course. But she couldn't stop smiling. Because for the first time, she knew that everything was going to be okay for them. For all of them.

CHAPTER 18

Rafe raised a hand to his brother before turning his full attention on his little mate. He was growling. He could feel it in his chest but he couldn't seem to stop. Not even as he watched Zoey walk away from Michael and towards him. Coming back to him, which filled him with relief but still didn't wipe out his irritation.

He'd been forced to let his mate go off with his brother. With his brother who loved her. And she loved him too. He could feel the warmth between them through the bond he had with them both. He could feel it like a thorn in his side that he knew would never go away, not fully. Because even though Zoey had made it clear she chose him, wanted him, the feelings she and Michael shared would never go away.

They were best friends. Family now. He'd heard her say that and it had made him want to smile and cringe at the same time.

It was one of the only things he'd heard because he'd had to put up with that asshole Enforcer glaring at him and making snide comments the whole time Zoey was talking to

Michael. In fact, the bastard had talked so much that Rafe had barely been able to catch any of his brother and his mate's conversation. He'd known Darius since they were all kids but they'd never been friends. Darius was usually a man of very few words and Rafe didn't doubt for a second that the bastard had only bothered talking to him to keep Rafe from eavesdropping.

He was a good Enforcer. He had Michael's back. Rafe could respect that. He still flipped him off as he climbed into the truck.

"Stop scowling at your brother." Zoey grinned as she bounded up the steps and straight into his arms.

He let out a rough breath and caught her. He pulled her in tight but the growl in his chest worked up his throat. She smelled all wrong. Like Michael. He scowled, hating it.

"Rafe." She giggled when he nuzzled his face into her throat. "That tickles."

"You smell like him." He growled in response and continued to rub himself against her.

"We only hugged."

"You should only ever smell like me."

Zoey giggled again, as if it were funny, but it wasn't funny. He was serious. Completely serious. He nuzzled her neck and stroked his hands over her body. He rubbed her against him, needing to remark her with his scent in every way. His wolf rubbed up against his skin and he groaned when he felt Zoey's pulse stutter and then race. He could feel her wolf respond too, lunge for the surface and she moaned too.

Done. He was done for. He hitched her up easily. Tiny little mate. Fit him so well. She wrapped her legs around his waist and he slipped his hands to her ass. He rubbed her against his already hardening cock, ignoring the engine that fired up in the drive as Darius and Michael left them alone. Zoey moaned.

"Wolves are sensitive to touch and smell." He gave into the urge to lick the pulse hammering in her neck, "No more hugging other men. You're mine."

Her arms tightened around his neck as she arched against him "Mmm, are you going to do this every time I come home with another male scent on me?"

He growled and she giggled again.

"Because if so, it's not really a threat." Her voice was breathy and she pulled on his hair, "Oh, God, Rafe, please... I want you. Please."

He grinned and nipped at her ear. His mate was perfect. Absolutely perfect. Beautiful and sassy too. Funny. Sweet. And his, all his.

"Need you."

It was the day of a full moon. It heightened both of their emotions. Good and bad. He knew that. But he didn't think it was just the moon making them want each other like this.

Everything between them was so new. Her wolf was newborn. The bond and the heat and everything that went along with being mated, with being a wolf, it was all so new. But it was strong, so damn strong.

He'd never been mated before so he couldn't know for sure but he thought it was more than just the bond, just their wolves. He couldn't get enough of her. Couldn't imagine he ever would.

He thought he was falling for her. Him. The man. It had nothing to do with his wolf. He was falling for this woman that made him feel so much, so easily. Made him feel like he could have everything he'd ever wanted.

Rafe turned and pushed her up against the side of the house. He took her mouth with his and she opened for him immediately. He would never get used to the kick of adrenaline when he tasted her sweetness. He wanted her on his tongue all the time, never wanted to taste anything that wasn't her.

Zoey writhed against him, breaking the kiss to gasp for air, "Rafe, please..."

Since he could hear the truck with the others down the road he knew they were far enough away not to see, he ripped the jacket she'd put on off her shoulders and pushed her shirt up. Her perfect little tits spilled out and he lowered his head to take a perky pink nipple into his mouth. She gasped his name and he sucked on her, hard.

He curled his tongue over the hard nub, "So damn responsive."

Rafe moved to her other breast and gave it the same treatment. He loved the way she moaned and sighed when he touched her. Loved that she writhed and begged for more. He loved these sweet little nipples, all red and standing at attention for him, loved the way her arousal spread a flush down her neck turning her pale skin pink.

It was gorgeous. She was gorgeous. The only way she would be more gorgeous was if... Rafe sank his teeth into the smooth curve of her breast.

"Rafe!" She screamed his name but it was more pleasure than pain and he groaned as he released the new mark and licked it. She was a wolf now. It healed almost instantly. But she'd have another silver scar to match the one on her neck. One only he would ever see.

"So sexy." He kissed the spot as she shivered in his arms, "Want to mark you everywhere."

"Please..." Zoey's head had fallen back against the wall, her eyes closed and her skin flushed, "Please, please, please..."

She was close. He could feel it. She was already shaking. Begging. She was still wearing those tiny little shorts so he slid his hand down her belly and beneath the waistband.

He growled, "So fuckin' wet. You need to come, baby?"

"Rafe." His name was a pleading whimper.

Her clit was so swollen he barely touched it and she cried out. So close. Too close. Because he wanted her to come while he was deep inside her. He needed to come with her. He needed to be buried inside her, filling her up with his seed. It was a pressing need on him, a weight he needed to fulfill. To make her his, to make them a family, to make them a pack.

"Not yet." He pulled his hand free and spun them around.

He sank onto the bench by the door with her in his lap. Zoey hissed and tugged at his shirt. He helped her push it off and then she abandoned the urge to undress him. He worked his pants open as she peppered him in frantic kisses.

She kissed his neck, his chest. She sucked on his nipples and tormented him the same way he'd tormented her. Her teeth scored his flesh and he groaned as a flare of need shot through him and his wolf clawed his insides. He wanted it. They both wanted it. Wanted their mate to mark them the same way they had marked her. But she couldn't shift yet, not until the full moon rose. No matter how much her wolf wanted it. She nipped at him but it wasn't enough. Not nearly enough.

Rafe shoved his pants out of the way and shifted her shorts to the side. He positioned himself with one hand and helped her lift up with the other. When she sank down on top of him, it was like finding home.

"Yes." He groaned as she took all of him with ease and

then gave a roll of her hips at the end. "Fuck me, baby. Ride me. Take me."

"Rafe." Her head fell back and her nails dug into his shoulders and she rocked herself on top of him.

Each time he was buried deep inside her, she rolled her hips, grinding her clit against him. Her movements were erratic and he knew she was close. So was he. He gripped her hips tight and helped her ride him and God, it felt good, so good. So right.

He took her breasts back in his mouth and she moved her claws to his hair. Her claws! He groaned when she scratched him. Her nails had elongated. Impossible. She couldn't change yet. Couldn't shift. She definitely couldn't control a half shift. He jerked back to look up at her and gasped.

Her eyes were gold. Her wolf was right there with him. With them. It shouldn't be possible but it was. Her wolf was strong. So damn strong. She was forcing her way to the surface. She wanted him that much.

"Do it." He growled as his own wolf clawed to get to her. "Do it baby. Mark me. You want it that bad? You take it."

Zoey whimpered and her jaw fell open. He knew it must have been confusing for her. Knew it probably hurt. He couldn't remember the first time he'd shifted, even a half shift, but it hurt when his teeth changed every damn time.

He leaned up and licked her longer canines, "Do it."

That earned him a growl and then Zoey bucked hard and sank her teeth into his pec. They both jolted and came. He could feel her body squeezing him as the orgasm roared through her. The tight grip of her pussy around him, the feel of her teeth in his chest, the mix of pleasure and pain and the howl of his wolf as his mate claimed him, it was too much to hold back. He jerked her down hard on top of him and held her there as he spilled his load deep inside of her.

He blacked out for a second. He was sure of it. It was the most intense orgasm of his life. He'd thought it couldn't get better than it had when he'd claimed her but this was better. Because she had chosen to claim him right back. Her wolf had fought to get to him. Rising to the surface when she shouldn't have been able to. Not yet.

Rafe groaned and held Zoey tight as they recovered their breath, "Baby?"

"Mmm." She moaned but didn't move from where she'd collapsed against his chest.

"You okay?"

"Mmm." She hummed again.

He couldn't decipher if that was a yes or a no so he wrapped a hand in her hair and pulled slightly. She harrumphed but curled upward when he tugged harder. He used his other hand to tip her chin up so she would look him in the eye and he breathed a sigh of relief when they were back to that beautiful green color.

"Are you okay?" He asked again, stroking her scalp soothingly where he'd pulled.

Her tongue ran over her teeth visibly and he waited. They'd gone back to normal already too. But there was a look of shock on her face that worried him and her pale skin was nearly ghostly. She swallowed hard and her eyes dropped to his chest, to the puncture marks that were already healing.

"I... I think so." She shivered and raised her hand to the mark, "Did I... I did that?"

"Your wolf did." Rafe spoke softly, soothingly, "She fought to the surface. You let her fight to the surface. You let her bite me."

Zoey's eyes darted back to his, "I claimed you."

His lips twitched slightly at the wonder in her, "You claimed me."

"You're mine." Her lips curled upward and he nodded as he wiped a spot of blood from her chin, "You're really mine."

"I'm yours baby. Always have been."

Zoey fell against his chest again, wrapping her arms around him and squeezing him tight. He wrapped his arms around her too. They'd just had sex on the front porch of the cabin. They were both nearly naked and disheveled. He was still buried inside her. And she'd claimed him.

His dick twitched.

She moaned and her hips automatically rocked into him, "Again?"

"Always." He licked his mark on her neck and she shivered, her body trembling with aftershocks. "I always want my little mate."

Zoey kissed the mark on his chest and sighed contently, "And I always want my big bad wolf."

He chuckled at that and felt his heart swell in his chest again. Laughter. He'd laughed more in the last twenty-four hours than he had in years. She made him smile. She made him laugh. She made him happy. And he was going to spend the rest of his life making her happy.

He flipped her onto her back on the bench and she moaned. He shifted above her, inside her, driving them both crazy. And when she met his eyes he gave her his biggest, wolfish grin.

"And this big bad wolf is gonna eat you up."

CHAPTER 19

R afe breathed in deeply and closed his eyes, relishing the scent of his mate all around him. All over him. That sweet, spicy scent that was pure Zoey. Only it was even better than that now. It was his scent and Zoey's mixed together. Their scent, the scent of a mated couple, covered them both and hung thick in the air around them. He couldn't get enough of it.

He was... happy. Content. He couldn't remember a time he'd ever felt so... right.

He pulled Zoey closer and she sleepily cuddled against his chest. They'd fallen back into bed together and he wasn't sure how much time had passed. Minutes. Hours. Days. He could spend eternity in this bed with his little mate but he knew that he couldn't , that they'd be interrupted again, sooner rather than later, which was why he couldn't sleep.

The full moon was coming. It was inching closer and closer the longer he laid here and did nothing. No, not nothing, he hugged Zoey closer and sniffed her hair. It calmed his wolf, who had been pacing beneath the surface of his skin for hours. He wasn't doing nothing. He was holding his mate. Comforting them both. Trying to mark her as thoroughly and deeply as possible so that when the wolf finally broke free he wouldn't ravage her.

"Rafe?" Zoey's voice was soft and sleepy as she nuzzled his chest.

"Shh, sleep baby."

"I... can't." Zoey groaned slightly and shifted, "You're holding me too tight."

He instantly loosened his hold, hating the idea of hurting her. He'd only been trying to protect her and he'd hurt her instead. What would happen if he couldn't protect her? Maybe he hadn't been build for it but he had to try.

He let go of her completely, "God, Zo, I'm sorry I..."

"It's okay." She kissed his chest lightly, "Hey. Hey. It's okay. Look at me."

He glanced down when she nudged at his chin and he met those beautiful green eyes of hers. There wasn't pain there. He hadn't actually hurt her. But there was confusion and more than a little bit of worry. He smoothed her hair back and tried to smile when she cuddled into the touch.

"What's wrong?"

"It's nothing."

"It's not nothing." She sighed, "Rafe, talk to me."

He'd learned her well enough to know that she wasn't going to let this go. She'd always been a stubborn one. He weighed the pros and cons, not wanting to fight with her, and finally did the only thing he could. He told her the truth.

"I never thought I'd have this."

Zoey's head tilted slightly, "Have what?"

"A home. A mate. You." Rafe twisted a lock of her hair around his finger, "I never thought I'd find you but, here you are and I'm... scared." He swallowed past the lump in his throat, "I hate that word. I hate admitting it but you're my mate and you need to know what's going on in my head. I'm scared, Zo. I'm scared that I'm going to lose you because I've done nothing to deserve you."

"Oh, Rafe..." Zoey's eyes softened, "Honey, no. You don't have to be scared of that. I'm not going anywhere."

"You can't know that."

"Michael isn't taking me away and I'm not..."

"That's not what I mean."

Zoey sat up, watching him through eyes that saw deep inside him, "Rafe... we talked about this. You're not going to hurt me. Your wolf isn't going to hurt me. I have my own wolf now and she'll defend herself if she has to but we both trust you. You're our mate and we're yours. It's going to be okay."

Rafe cupped her cheeks and pulled her close, taking her mouth in a soft, sweet kiss. Zoey returned it just the same. She melted into him and he pulled her onto his lap. He threaded his fingers into her hair and slicked his tongue into her mouth. He kept kissing her until he was certain that neither of them had any air left and she knew just how crazy he was about her.

She was amazing. Incredible. And she was his. His mate. His forever. To honor and cherish and most of all, to protect.

He wouldn't fail her. Not her. Not now and not ever.

"You're too good for me." He gasped against her lips as he held her close.

"No. I'm perfect for you. That's why I'm your mate." Zoey smiled softly, pressing sweet kisses along his jaw.

"You read my mind."

She laughed softly, the most melodic sound he'd ever

heard and pushed his hair back gently, "I don't read your mind, Rafe. I don't have to. Everything you think is right here on your gorgeous face."

He let her trace every inch of his face and held still for her. Her fingers were soft and smart, following the lines of his forehead and cheeks. She dipped down along his jaw and the crease of his chin and then, finally, she traced his lips which automatically curled upwards into a smile.

"What am I thinking right now, little mate?"

Zoey smirked, "You're thinking how lucky you are that fate gave me to you as a mate."

"I am. I'm so lucky." He pulled her head slightly until she bent down and he could kiss her again. "What else?"

That earned him another laugh, "Oh, that one's easy." Her hips shifted slightly, "Or should I say, hard?" he put his hands on her hips to hold her against his erection, "You want me again."

"I always want you." He nibbled on her earlobe.

"Mmm..." She sighed contentedly and then surprised him by pulling away, "But you'll have to hold that thought, mate. I need to take a shower and then go check on the bakery. It's always busy the day of a full moon and.... HEY!"

Zoey squealed in protest when he rolled her underneath him and growled.

He was hearing things. He must be. Either that or he'd actually managed to fall asleep and this was a dream. A nightmare. Because there was no way in the world he'd actually just heard his new mate tell him that she intended to leave him to go to work on the day of a full moon. The first full moon after she'd become his. The first full moon that she would experience with a wolf of her own. There was no way she honestly thought she was leaving him. No way.

"Rafe, what the..."

"You're not going anywhere." He growled and his wolf hissed his agreement.

"Rafe..." Her voice was a warning but he ignored it with a snarl.

"I'm not letting you out of my sight, Zo. Not today. Not tomorrow. Not ever."

His wolf was already pacing at the very idea. He wouldn't lose her. He couldn't. He'd only just found her.

Zoey frowned, "Rafe... listen to me."

"Zo..."

"No!" She raised her voice and met his eyes seriously, "You listen to me. You can't keep me locked up out here. I'm not a prisoner. I'm your mate."

"I know that. It's why I need to protect you." Rafe winced when his wolf clawed at his insides, "I can't lose you. Zo, baby, I can't lose you."

Zoey softened underneath him and he breathed a sigh of relief. She was going to see reason. She was going to understand. She was his mate. She had to. On some soul deep level she had to understand that after all he'd lost, the very idea of letting her go and having something happen to her would kill him. He'd lost the last shreds of his sanity and there would be no coming back from it this time.

"Oh, Rafe..." Zoey softly swiped his hair back again, "You're not going to lose me. I promise."

"Zo, you can't..."

"You can't keep me as a prisoner. I have a life. I have a bakery that I own and I run. I have a family that is going to want to see me, to hear what happened and see for themselves that I'm okay. You told Michael you wouldn't take me from my life here but that's exactly what you'll be doing if you lock me up out here."

Rafe shook his head, "I'm not... I can't..."

"I won't abide it, Rafe. It's best you get it out of your head right now. I'm not some timid little thing that's going to let you get away with putting me on a pedestal to keep me safe. I'm going to live my life the same way I always have. I want you to be a part of it."

Everything inside of him felt like it was bleeding. His wolf was ripping at his organs and his skin. He hated the thought of losing her but more than that he realized that he hated the idea of hurting her. And he knew that keeping her away from the world would hurt her. She was right. She had a family and a life and he didn't want to take them from her. He wanted to be a part of that life with her.

But God, just the thought of her going out there in the world alone, even if it was just Noir, the safest place she could possibly be, he could barely breathe.

"Rafe..." Zoey tilted his chin up and he realized that he'd dropped his head and closed his eyes in agony, "Rafe, honey, look at me. Please?"

"Zo..."

"I know this is hard for you. I understand why." Zoey was stroking his hair, petting and soothing him and his animal both, "What you went through, losing your parents and Gabe, I know you'll never get past it. I'm not asking you to. But I am asking that you trust me on this, I won't put myself in any unnecessary danger. I won't ever leave you by choice and I know that you'll never let anything happen to me if you can help it. But you have to let me go and trust that I'll come back to you. I'll always come back to you."

He swallowed past the knot in his throat, "You can't promise that you'll come back. That's out of your power. That's in fate's hands and..."

"Exactly. Exactly, Rafe. It's in fate's hands, not mine

and not yours. We'll have as much time together as fate allows and we both have to trust that it's going to be a really, really long time. That we're going to get to grow old together, have pups together and raise them together."

"I want that."

"I know." Zoey leaned up and kissed him softly, "I know. I want that too. But what kind of life will it be if I can't leave this cabin? Think about it. Logically. Be reasonable. I know you want to protect me but you have to be reasonable Rafe."

The thing was, logically, rationally, he knew that keeping her locked up here was unreasonable. He knew it was impossible. She was too strong to allow it, to allow him to control her that way. But the unreasonable side of him, his wolf side, was going crazy at the idea of letting her out of his sight.

The last time he'd let someone he loved out of his sight, they'd all been slaughtered like animals.

"Zo..." He winced and shook his head.

He didn't know what to do. It was something he could work on. He could promise her that. But he couldn't do it today. He couldn't let her go today. Not today. Not when she was just barely his and his wolf hadn't properly claimed her yet. Not fully. Not on a full moon.

"How about we compromise for now?"

He sucked in a surprised breath and studied her face, curious what she could possibly mean, "What?"

"I know that it's going to take some time and some adjustments on both of our parts to make this relationship work but it's what we both want right?"

He nodded instantly and the pain in his chest eased a little when she smiled up at him.

"So we compromise." Zoey stroked his cheek, "I need to

go into town and you can't bear to be away from me so you'll come with me."

"I..." He stuttered and tilted his head, "I didn't know that was an option."

"It won't always be. I won't have you stalking around me like a bodyguard all the time, Rafe. But you're my mate and it's a full moon and I understand why you're worried. So for today, you can accompany me to town while I run my errands, okay?"

He fought the hot liquid that built behind his eyes. His mate was so sweet. So sweet and smart and understanding. She was giving him what he needed, just like a good mate should. He could give her what she needed too. In time, he would be able to loosen his hold, at least he hoped that he could. He was a born Alpha. He was a dominant shifter. She was his mate. He would always want to keep her close and protect her. But he would learn how to loosen his grip without losing his sanity. Someday.

"You'd do that?" He managed to choke out.

"Of course I will." Zoey wiped at his cheek and he realized a tear had slipped from the corner of his eye, "You mean everything to me. I want to make you happy and I want you to be part of my life. Not just here in the cabin but everywhere. You're my mate, Rafe. So come to town with me and let me show my hot, sexy, Alpha mate off to my friends would you?"

He hadn't thought it was possible but he snorted a laugh, "You want to... show me off?"

"Mmhmm." Zoey rubbed up against him and coyly batted her lashes, "I have a hot born Alpha mate that makes me wet just breathing. I want all those bitches in the pack to know that you're mine and I'll claw their eyes out if they so much as look at you for too long."

Rafe nuzzled her neck and the mark he'd put there, "One condition."

"Hmm?"

"No shower before we go. I want my scent all over you if we're going to town. Want all those males to know you're mine and I won't just claw their eyes out, I'll rip out their throats if they put a finger on you."

"Mmm." Zoey hummed happily, "How is it sexy when you talk like a homicidal maniac? Is that a bond thing or a mate thing or am I just into super possessive crazy guys?"

He chuckled again, ignoring her question, "Do we have a deal?"

"Deal." She nodded and arched when he slid a hand down to cup her breast, "Oh, God, Rafe... we don't have time."

"We're skipping showers." He reminded her, his lips following the trail his hand took down her body, "We have plenty of time."

"But the... Ohhhhhh!" Zoey moaned, her hands going to his hair as he knelt between her legs and put his mouth on her.

Rafe grinned against her soft pink flesh. His. She was all his. They'd had their first argument and they'd reached a compromise. He fully intended to show her how happy that made him. That they could work together, find a way to fit their lives together. He dipped his head and suckled, taking her flavor onto his tongue and feeling his wolf relax with the knowledge that he would be able to keep her close all day.

She was already theirs and when the moon rose tonight... they'd make it official.

CHAPTER 20

"**S**top it."

Rafe's hand tightened on hers and she shot apologetic looks to the three men that had just crossed the street to avoid them. Luckily they were pack and they must have understood because they lowered their gazes and didn't glance back once. She let out an uneasy breath, thankful they hadn't taken Rafe's growling as an excuse to start a fight.

"Stop what?" His voice was low as he tugged her against his side and nuzzled her hair.

"Growling at literally every person we see." She softened slightly at the affectionate gesture and squeezed his hand reassuringly, "Nobody here is a threat to me."

"I don't like them looking at you."

Zoey glanced up to see his mouth curve into an adorably sexy pout and hid a smile against his shoulder, "They're not looking at me, Rafe. They're looking at you because you're emitting a low-key warning growl like a bomb about to go off. Now cut it out before we get to the shop because if you scare all my customers away I'm going to be pissed."

"The men were looking at you." He insisted.

She sighed, "So what if they were?"

"You're mine."

"Exactly. I'm yours. They can look if they want but all they're going to see is how much I want my mate. You."

"I warned you what would happen if one of them touches you..."

"And nobody will touch me but you." Zoey cut him off with a shake of her head, trying to reassure him for what felt like the millionth time since they left the cabin, "I chose you. Remember?"

Rafe's throat bobbed as he swallowed, "I don't want you to regret that. I know I'm... overbearing."

"You're protective." Zoey stopped walking and faced him, "You're also sweet and sexy and you're mine. I don't want to share you with the world any more than you want to share me. But our life is here and we have to live it. We talked about this."

"I know." Rafe's free hand came up and gently traced the mark on her neck, sending goosebumps racing over her skin and heat straight to her core, "I'm just on edge about tonight. The full moon and my wolf and..."

Zoey caught his hand and brought it to her lips, kissing his knuckles softly, "Let's not worry about tonight right now. Let's just focus on getting through the day. Okay?"

"Okay." Rafe finally nodded.

She went up on tiptoe and brushed her lips against his. Rafe immediately growled and swept down to claim her mouth. He hauled her against him and the heat between them sparked. She opened her mouth when his tongue demanded entry and whimpered when he teased her with it, pumping in and out in a filthy, suggestive way that made her want him inside her so bad she ached.

"Holy. Fucking. Shit."

The words snapped her out of her fantasy and back to reality. Where she and Rafe were making out on the sidewalk just in front of her bakery. Where people were walking past and cars were driving by. Where her assistant and friend was gaping at them with wide-mouthed astonishment from barely two feet away.

Zoey felt her cheeks flush and began to disentangle herself, "Uh, hey April."

Her friend's eyes stayed glued to Rafe , unblinking for a long moment before she shook her head and glanced back at Zoey, "I heard the rumors I just... I thought Michael... I didn't believe... holy fucking shit."

Zoey managed a slight chuckle and nodded to the stuttering woman, "Rafe, soak it in. You've officially left April Warner speechless, a feat I thought was impossible." Her friend managed to pull her jaw shut and Zoey continued, "April, you remember Rafe Hudson right?"

"Right. Yeah. How could I forget?" April fidgeted slightly, looking between them, "So you two are really... like... together then?"

"Mated." Zoey nodded and squeezed Rafe's hand when he remained stock still at her side. "Rafe's my mate."

April looked even more astonished at the confirmation, as if that had even seemed possible, "Well, uh, congratulations. And... welcome back to Noir, Rafe."

"Warner." Rafe finally spoke, his head tilting slightly, "You're Ethan's... sister?"

"Ouch." April blinked and laughed, "No. Ethan's sister is Isla and she's about ten years older than me. I'm Ethan's mate."

"April used to be a Kellogg before she mated with Ethan." Zoey tried to dig her new mate out of the hole he'd stepped into.

"Oh... yes. Sorry." Rafe ran his free hand through his dark hair, ducking his head a little in apology, "You were younger than me in school but I remember your brother. Anderson. We were friends. Is he still in town?"

April nodded, "He is. He's a deputy now and he's also an Enforcer for the pack."

"Like Michael couldn't have brought him this morning then?" Rafe growled low, just for Zoey's ears, "But no, he had to bring that other bastard. Figures."

"Okay so..." Zoey chirped, ignoring Rafe's latest reason to fight with his brother, "Now that introductions are over, how about we stop making a scene on the sidewalk and go inside? God knows I could use a cup of coffee."

"Me too." April nodded enthusiastically, "I'm basically an invalid until I get some caffeine in my system."

"After you, ladies." Rafe stepped forward quickly and grabbed the door.

Zoey shot her friend a reassuring smile when April flinched at his sudden movement. She knew Rafe was big and he didn't exactly come off as friendly. But she was hoping that this trip into town would convince people he wasn't quite the animal he'd made himself out to be last night. From the looks of it, she had her work cut out for her since April hadn't even been at that party.

"Ladies?" Rafe prompted when April still didn't move and Zoey rolled her eyes and shoved her friend.

"April. Stop staring. Go. Now." She pushed her friend through the door and tugged Rafe in behind her.

"Sorry. Sorry. I..." April finally got moving and they stumbled into the bakery, which promptly went silent.

Zoey cringed and her friend gave an apologetic shrug as if she'd known this would happen. Which, maybe Zoey should have known as well. She'd expected there would be gossip in town. She'd known they would get looks and questions after the way everything had gone down last night. But back at the cabin everything had felt so right between her and Rafe that she'd convinced herself they'd be okay out here, in public. Maybe Rafe had been right. Maybe they should have stayed home today and let the rumors die down. Maybe...

"Rafe, my boy!" An older man that sat in the back got to his feet and started towards them with a big, welcoming smile on his face, "It's so nice to see you."

"Mr. Lang." Rafe offered his free hand as the man got closer.

"Oh, come now, I think you're old enough to call me Richard now." The former high school science teacher all but beamed as he glanced at Zoey, "And good morning to you as well. Getting a late start I see."

Zoey felt the blush heat her cheeks and to her utter shock and amusement, heard Rafe chuckle. That sound. Her insides bloomed with warmth and pleasure. She forgot all about how awkward the conversation with April had been outside. Forgot that her old teacher had basically just called her out for her tardiness. She simply basked in the sound of Rafe enjoying himself.

"It was my fault."

"I had no doubt about that, son." Richard Lang chuckled as well, "Why don't you come sit with me and we can catch up? Let Ms. Zoey get to work."

She gave the older man a grateful smile for the offer, for his show of kindness. He'd always been a nice man. He'd been a good teacher, stern but helpful. As one of her regulars, he all but kept her in business buying up boxes of treats every morning during the school year for his group of retired friends. She was thankful he'd made the gesture to welcome Rafe when everyone else was still staring and whispering but she didn't expect her mate to take him up on it until he squeezed her hand and then loosened his grip.

"He's right. I should let you get to work. It's why we're here after all."

She felt her heart thump as she looked up into those gorgeous dark eyes of his, "Are you sure?"

"I'm sure." Rafe leaned down and brushed his lips over hers gently, "I'll be right here if you need me and you'll try to stay where I can see you. Right?"

Zoey nodded instantly because the thickness in her throat kept her from words. He was trying. He was really trying. For her. Compromise. He'd come to town even though he didn't want to. He would take a seat in the café and let her get some work done. She knew it wouldn't be easy for him to be apart from her, even that small distance, but he was trying.

She launched herself into his arms, hugging him tight and felt his answering smile against the top of her head as he caught her. Oh God, her heart ached. She was falling for him. Fast and crazy and she didn't think it was only because of the heat or the bond or the wolves. It was because he was Rafe. Handsome and kind, sweet and sexy, protective and damaged but trying... for her. And she knew right then and there that her heart didn't stand a chance.

She was falling in love with her mate.

"Go." Rafe whispered against her ear, "Before I change my mind and haul you back to our bed."

She grinned, "Tonight."

A low growl vibrated through his chest and he pulled

back and kissed her soundly before shoving her gently away, "Go to work, Zo. The sooner you finish the sooner we can get out of here."

Zoey blew him a kiss before taking a deep breath and turning her back on him to walk away. It felt strange not touching him when she'd spent nearly every minute of the last twelve hours in his arms. She wanted to rush back to him as soon as the distance grew by more than a few feet but she forced herself on, knowing it was an important step in their relationship that they move it out of the bedroom and into the world.

Knowing she was testing her limits and his, she stepped through the swinging door into the kitchen to grab her apron. As soon as she did, she bore down, expecting him to come striding through the doors behind her. When a few seconds passed and he didn't, she finally released the breath she had been holding and looked up to find her pastry chef staring at her.

"Good morning." She grinned at her mother.

"Good morning?" Laura Kent's eyebrows hit her hairline and she laughed as she dusted her hands on her own apron, "That's all I get? Good morning? My only daughter goes to a party, starts a fight between the Pack Alpha and his long lost brother, disappears with a feral wolf and then walks back in here covered in his scent, mated no less, and all I get is a good morning?"

Zoey giggled, "Well, when you put it like that... good morning Mama. There's something I should tell you..."

"Oh, you silly, silly, girl. You went and found yourself a mate." Her mother crossed the distance between them with her arms open, "And you didn't even think to call and tell your father or me."

"I'm sorry." Zoey stepped into the loving embrace, "Things have been a little hectic and Rafe..."

Her mother jolted and gasped. Laura jerked back from the hug she'd bestowed on her daughter. Here eyes were wide and her cheeks had gone pale. Her dark eyes, so unlike Zoey's own, raced over her from top to bottom before finally settling on the silver scar that graced the spot where her neck and shoulder met.

"Oh Zozo." She whispered softly, worriedly, as she slowly raised a hand and touched the mark.

"I told you there was something I needed to tell you." Zoey whispered back, catching her mother's hand and twining their fingers, "I have a wolf now."

"Oh, baby." Laura pulled her daughter back into her arms and squeezed her so tight Zoey could barely breathe. "I know how much you've wanted this. For so long, so very long, I've watched you hurt because it wasn't Michael. Please, please just tell me that you're happy with the mate the fate's gave you."

"I'm happy, Mama." Zoey felt tears fill her eyes and sniffled slightly, "I have a mate and a wolf now and... I think I'm falling in love with him. Just like you and Daddy did."

"Oh my sweet baby girl. That's all I've ever wanted for you." Laura pulled back and wiped at her own cheeks, which were streaked with tears, "He's a good match then?"

"The best."

"I've been trying not to jump to conclusions with all the gossip but you know they've been talking about him. The True Alpha that came back and fought the Pack Alpha for his mate? They said Michael didn't take it well. I can't imagine it was easy for any of you, not with the connection you and he have always shared."

"It was rough, to say the least." Zoey admitted, "Not

just for Michael and me but for Rafe too. It wasn't like he expected it any more than we did but it makes sense right? The connection to Michael I've always felt. It's because we're family now."

"Family." Her mother brushed her hair back softly and smiled, "Those boys need some family and I'm overjoyed that we get to be it now. Just so long as my baby is happy, I'm happy."

"Thank you Mama."

"So..." Laura dabbed at her hair and then dusted her apron, "Do I get to meet my only daughter's mate now? I haven't seen that boy since he was barely old enough to be called a man. I'd like to meet the wolf that gave my girl everything she ever wanted."

Zoey winced at the expectation that was all too reasonable, "Uh... maybe, if you wouldn't mind, we could... wait?"

"Wait?"

"It's just that, he's really protective. Reclusive even. Getting him to come to town was an ordeal and I'm not sure he's in the right frame of mind to meet my mom just yet, considering... everything."

Laura's eyes softened, "You mean considering that I was best friends with his mother before she passed?"

Zoey nodded.

"You think it'll bring back bad memories for him?" Her mother sighed and played with her hair again, "You're a good mate for him Zo. Looking after him. If that's what you think is best, then I'll give you two some time before I insist he meet with your father and I. I'll stay back here out of sight for now."

"Thank you Mama. I'm so sorry to ask it of you I just... I don't want to hurt him."

"I hope he knows how lucky he is, my darling."

"He does." The rough voice came from the doorway and Zoey sucked in a gasp of air as she spun to face Rafe.

He looked more than a little awkward, his big frame taking up most of the swinging doorframe. He also looked apologetic. His dark eyes swung from her to her mother and then to the floor. He shifted uncomfortably and his big shoulders shrugged.

"I felt... something. I didn't know what it was. Worry? I thought you might need me." He glanced back up and met her eyes, "I'm sorry to interrupt. I know I said I'd stay out there I just... I thought something was wrong."

Zoey's heart did that melting thing again and she stepped away from her mother, offering her hand to Rafe who quickly covered the distance between them, sweeping her into his arms and nuzzling her reassuringly. Worry. He'd felt her worry. Only it hadn't been for herself. It had been for him. He'd felt her emotions through the bond and that connection would only get stronger the longer they had together.

"I'm sorry. I'm fine." She whispered reassuringly as she swept her hands over his back.

"You were worried... for me?" He leaned back enough to look down at her and she nodded when she saw the confusion and then amazement cross his features. "I'm supposed to be the overprotective one."

That made her grin, "You protect me. I protect you. Compromise, remember?"

"Sweet little mate." Rafe brushed his lips over her forehead, her cheeks and then her lips.

Her mother cleared her throat and Zoey pulled away from the embrace with another blush. She glanced up but Rafe only nodded. She wasn't sure how much he'd heard. With his special wolf hearing, maybe he'd heard all of it. It didn't matter. What mattered was that he was here, with her, and there was only one thing she could do now.

"Rafe, I'd like you to meet my mother, Laura Kent."

His throat bobbed slightly, "Mrs. Kent..."

"Oh, honey, I think its just Laura from now on." Her mother smiled warmly.

"It's nice to see you again... Laura." Rafe nodded, "And I want to thank you for bring Zoey into my life. Your daughter is my perfect mate in every way and I'll do my damndest to be good for her in return."

Zoey's eyes watered again as her mother opened her arms. Rafe hesitated for only a moment. In the next breath, he'd taken two strides and was stooping to hug her mother in return. Zoey watched the two of them and felt her heart swell with love and pride. This was just the beginning of what they would share, of what being together would be able to fix for Rafe and she had no doubt that he would keep his word. He would do everything he could to be the best mate for her, because he already was.

Laura released him with a rough pat on the back and Rafe stood back to his full height. Her mother wiped at her cheeks again and then reached up and cupped Rafe's cheek. She held him there, small but firm and met his eyes when she spoke again.

"Welcome to the family."

CHAPTER 21

It was almost time. Zoey could feel it. As the day had progressed, she'd felt her wolf get stronger and stronger.

About mid-day, they'd had to leave the bakery because she couldn't concentrate. The itch under her skin had been bearable but only when Rafe had been touching her, soothing her and coaxing her into relaxing. Next had come the fever, the rush of heat that had made her sweat and then chill and then sweat again. The same heat that had made her all but crawl up Rafe's body looking for relief. And all day he'd been right there for her, with her, promising her that once the moon was up, high in the sky, that she'd feel better.

It had been a weird day and considering she was standing in the middle of the woods with her mate who had just stripped his clothes off and turned into a wolf in front of her eyes, it was strange to think it was about to get even weirder.

She was going to turn into a wolf. Her. She wasn't

human anymore. She was special, just like she'd always wanted to be, but she was also terrified.

Rafe rubbed against her leg, bringing her thoughts back to the present and she couldn't help but smile down at him. He was a beautiful wolf. A beautiful wolf for a beautiful man. He was big but she'd expected that. He was a born Alpha. His wolf was huge and muscular and if she'd come across him alone in the woods she'd have screamed her head off. His coat was as black as midnight and his eyes shone like diamonds in the night. Considering how worried he'd been about his wolf freaking out and attacking her, she couldn't help but smile when she reached down to pet him and he all but purred.

He'd shifted first only after a lot of discussion and she was glad that he had. Now they both knew the truth. His wolf would never hurt her. He adored her, just like she adored him. He paced around her in circles, his head going back and forth as if he was searching for threats and only when he was sure that they were still alone, did he turn back to her and bark.

She smiled when he bounced around a little. She knew what he wanted. He wanted to play, but not with her. He wanted her wolf. He wanted her to shift.

Zoey took a deep breath and let it out. She shook her hands out and tried to steady her breathing. They'd talked this through. Rafe had told her how to do it. He'd told her how to open her mind up and let the wolf come to the forefront. It's what her wolf wanted so it would be easy. That's what he'd said.

"Okay, baby, here goes nothing." She whispered softly and then closed her eyes.

She focused on the feel of her wolf just beneath her skin. The power in her veins. The scent of her mate in her nose. The feel of fur and claws. She breathed deeply, evenly, and simply let go of her skin, let go of all her doubts and fears and worries. She let go of herself and let her wolf take control.

And then she screamed.

She was shifting and it hurt. Oh, holy hell it hurt. She felt every single break of her bones. She felt her muscles tear and pull as they reshaped. She screamed again as her body convulsed and she cursed Rafe for telling her this was going to be easy. This was the opposite of easy. This was killing her and never, not once in all of her dreams of becoming a wolf had she given a thought to how it would feel to shift.

She'd been human. She hadn't been allowed on the pack land at the lodge on full moon nights. It had been for her safety. That's what Michael had said. But she thought it might also have been because he hadn't wanted her to know just how difficult a transition really was.

It was like being ripped apart. Inch by inch. Piece by piece. She lost a little more of herself with every heaving breath.

The world around her dimmed and turned blurry. Everything shimmered and shook. She thought she was losing her mind too. Losing her sanity. The only tether to the real world that she had was Rafe. He was there with her, just like he'd promised. His wolf paced and rubbed against her. He whined as if seeing her in pain was hurting him and she tried to reach for him. She wanted to pet him, reassure him that she was okay, but when she reached out her hand... it wasn't there.

Zoey tried to scream again but instead all she heard was a howl.

She blinked, blinked again and her surroundings began

to come into focus all around her again. She was closer to the ground now and everything looked different from down here. Sharper. Brighter. Her eyes looked through the forest around her as if it was broad daylight instead of dark. And she could smell everything. The damp grass and the rot of leaves. She could hear them crunch and crackle and her head whipped up to find what had caused the sound. When her eyes met those of Rafe's wolf, she felt all of those broken pieces of her click back into place.

Zoey's wolf shook herself, stretching and pawing at the ground and then bared her teeth playfully. Rafe's wolf barked and hers yipped in return. Zoey's heart swelled all over again. She wanted to launch herself at him. She wanted to press against him and cuddle with him. But there was something her wolf wanted more, something she needed on this night, her first night fully in the world.

She yipped again and took off running.

A long, loud howl sounded behind her but she didn't pause and she didn't look back. Her advanced hearing told her all she needed to know. Pounding footfalls raced after her. Rafe was chasing her. She ran, all out, as fast as she could. Her newly formed wolf leaping over logs and twining through trees but Rafe stayed right there with her. Behind her, beside her, nipping at her heels and spurring her on. She knew he could have caught her at any time. He was an Alpha. He was bigger. He was older. His wolf was more powerful and far faster. But he let her run and he... played... with her.

She swore as they darted through trees, playing hide and seek, that she heard him laugh. Even in wolf form, she knew that sound and she loved it. She loved this. She loved that she was finally a wolf. Loved that Rafe was the one that had given it to her. Loved the connection she felt to him like this and the freedom she felt under the moon. She loved that he could be like this with her. Sweet and playful and fun.

She lost all track of time as they played and ran through the forest. His wolf was always right there with her. When she got too close to the edge of their territory he herded her back the other direction. When she caught scent of another animal and went to check it out, he shooed the deer away before her wolf could do something she'd regret in the morning.

He took care of her. Looked after her. Protected her and cherish her. Just like he'd sworn that he would.

And when he'd finally had enough, when he decided that he'd let her play enough, she felt his mood switch before he ever came after her. His growl lowered, became darker, and she leaped away when he pawed at her. His wolf hissed and came at her again but her wolf wasn't submissive. She didn't intend to go down without a fight even if she knew that he was their mate. She hissed right back at him and then took off again at full speed, knowing that this time he wouldn't let her get away with it and falling even more in love with him when he gave a happy yip of encouragement and gave chase again.

She headed straight for the meadow, their meadow, and the instant she hit the wide-open space he was on her. He leaped and took her down easily. They rolled as he tackled her. Paws tangling but with their claws safely sheathed. Their tongues were both lolling and they were panting by the time he pinned her beneath him.

Zoey smiled. Her wolf hummed a happy, contented sound and gave up the faux fight. She relaxed beneath her mate and when her head rolled to the side, exposing her neck, Rafe's wolf howled a sound that couldn't be mistaken for anything but satisfaction.

It was time. Finally. Zoey's heart rate sped up as she stared into those glowing golden eyes. They weren't just wolf eyes. They were Rafe's eyes. The eyes of her mate. Her other half and the male that would complete her. He'd already given her so much and now, she was going to give him this. She gave a small nod and his wolf lowered his head.

His thick, scratchy tongue tickled as he licked at her. Caressing her. Marking her before he took her. She didn't budge. She didn't move. She wanted him to know that she trusted him completely. Him and his wolf. She trusted that he wouldn't hurt her. That this was the right thing, the only thing, because they were mates.

He had to complete the circle to bond them forever.

Rafe's wolf licked her again and she whined and snapped at him. He was taking too long and she could feel the tension coming off of him in waves. He was holding back. He was holding his wolf back. He was still scared that he would hurt her. She bared her teeth and nipped at him again, catching at his skin and hoping he would get the hint that she was ready.

She trusted him. Completely.

Rafe's wolf growled at her. He bared his teeth when she arched her neck. He dropped his head back and howled long and loud at the full moon over their head and then, faster than she could even comprehend he snapped forward and dug his teeth into the flesh of her neck, right where her shoulder met, right where he'd marked her in human form.

It was rougher. Wilder than anything she'd ever imagined. His wolf took hers and sealed the bond in place.

Forged it in fire and blood. Unbreakable. They were mates now and nothing could ever come between them.

Zoey's wolf howled right along with him. Finally, she was whole. Finally, she was home. She was, finally, who she was always meant to be. Thanks to Rafe. Her beautiful, twisted, born Alpha wolf mate.

CHAPTER 22

Rafe couldn't remember a time his wolf had ever been so content. Docile even. He was happy. Here, on his own soil, on pack soil, with her, he finally felt like he'd come home.

God, she was the most beautiful thing he'd ever seen. Her wolf looked a lot like her. Small and lean with red and white coloring, she was Zoey in wolf form. Perfection. Sassy and fun, playful and energetic but she had a calming effect on him too. She was perfect and his wolf was absolutely crazy about her.

He couldn't stop nuzzling her. Licking her. Loving her. He'd taken her multiple times already. So many times that he worried he should have warned her about what could happen on a full moon, especially a first full moon when a wolf's hormones were the highest.

He hadn't thought about it before. He'd been too worried about the bad things that could happen to think about the good. He'd been worried that he would hurt her. Worried his wolf would maul her. He'd worried about how the change would effect her and if she would be hurting after the change. He'd thought about ways he could take care of her after, tomorrow, when they changed back into their human forms and she would need rest.

But he hadn't so much as given a thought to the fact that his new mate would be highly fertile tonight and that his wolf would see it as his duty, no, his mission, to take her over and over again until she was pregnant with his pups.

Rafe's wolf growled at the thought and cuddled in closer to her. They'd just finished another round of love-making and were lazing about in the field. Enjoying the simple feel of one another. Their wolves tired from all the playing and sex. But just the thought of Zoey pregnant with his pups made his wolf stir with need again.

Lord, he really should have warned her. Even now, there could be new life growing in her belly. Pregnancy was always dangerous for a shifter. It would be especially difficult for a new wolf to control the shifts and keep the pups safe. He would need help protecting her if that was the case. He'd need a medic or a midwife and he would need the pack.

Rafe's wolf twitched at the thought. Michael had told him that they weren't part of the Moirae pack. He'd said Rafe's wolf had broken ties to the land because he'd been gone too long. He'd thought that was true. The proof was in Zoey's wolf. Michael hadn't sensed her and she hadn't sensed him, not on an Alpha level. But from the moment he'd shifted, he'd felt the pull of the pack.

He didn't understand it. Couldn't figure it out. Not in his wolf form. It was something he'd have to talk to Michael about after the full moon waned. Because Moirae pack or not, he was still tied to this land and he thought it was because he was still tied to Michael. They were brothers.

They might have their differences. They might both be born Alphas. They might want to fight for dominance. But the truth of the matter was, when it mattered, when it counted, his wolf would always see this place as home because Noir was where Michael was and he was the only family Rafe had left.

Zoey nuzzled against him and he amended the thought. Not anymore. He had her now. He had her sweet mother who had welcomed him with open arms. He had a brother and a mate and a pack. He was sure of it.

A prickle of unease raised the hair on the back of his neck and his wolf whined. Rafe blinked and whipped his head around, looking for a threat. When he saw none, he shook the feeling off. He was just being nervous. He was on edge because he was in wolf form on pack land for the first time since he lost his family. He was uneasy because he didn't just have himself to worry about anymore. He had Zoey and maybe, possibly, the pups she was already growing inside her.

His family.

But Rafe couldn't shake the feeling of unease when it hit him again and his wolf leapt up, pacing. Zoey whined and shook herself. Her head tilted and a low growl came from deep in her throat. Rafe watched her look around as well, stalking upright into a defensive position.

And it clicked, just like that, just that fast.

He wasn't crazy. He wasn't being overprotective. Zoey felt it too. She knew something was off but she couldn't place what it was either. There was no immediate threat to them. They were alone in this part of the woods, out by the lake and near their cabin, which meant...

There was only one other thing that connected their wolves. That would make both of them nervous and worried. One thing, one person, that both of them loved and would want to protect as much in their wolf forms and they would in their human forms.

Michael.

Panic welled inside of him. Something was wrong. Something was wrong with Michael. His wolf howled in pain and Zoey's wolf winced. He felt like he was being torn in half. The need to stay here and be with her and make sure she was okay and the urge to race to his brother, to his only living blood relative.

Somewhere, in the distance, another wolf answered his howl of pain and recognition hit Rafe in the gut like a bullet, ripping away his last shreds of sanity.

That was Michael. It was Michael howling and he was in pain. He was hurt and with that sound a hundred other awful memories surged. The sound of his other brother in pain. Gabe dying. His parents dead. Now Michael.

No. No. No. His wolf took off. He didn't stop or pause or look back. He couldn't hear anything but the sound of his blood pounding in his ears and the echo of that howl. No. Not Michael. He couldn't lose Michael too. He'd only just gotten him back. No. No. No.

He didn't think. Couldn't think. All he could do was run. As fast as he could, he ran towards the pack land at the lodge. It was the direction he'd heard Michael's howl come from and he assumed it was the place where the pack still grouped together on full moons to shift together.

It was a couple of miles away but he ran. He ran as fast as he could. Leaping over logs. Dodging trees. And somewhere, in the back of his mind, he knew that Zoey was behind him, that she was racing after him as steadily as he was racing towards Michael. But he couldn't stop and he couldn't slow down.

Not when Michael was in pain.

He didn't know how long it took but as soon as he got close to the lodge, he scented it. He wasn't crazy. He wasn't panicking for no reason. He could smell blood in the air. Pack blood. Moirae blood. Michael's blood.

And his wolf lost his mind just as surely as the man inside of him did when he saw what was happening.

The attack that he'd warned his brother about. It was happening. Here and now. The pack was under attack and Rafe hadn't been here. He hadn't been here to help Michael. To protect Michael. His only brother. His pack. He hadn't been here to protect them just like he hadn't been there to protect Gabe and their parents.

All over the place, there were wolves fighting. Claws and teeth, growling and hissing. He didn't recognize any of the wolves. He had no idea who was who but there were some he could sense. They were pack. They were Moirae and he could sense them because he had Moirae blood and he was tied to the pack. Something inside of him snapped into place and his vision blurred before it focused back in and he saw Michael.

Michael. His brother. His Pack Alpha.

Rafe jumped into the fight, viciously swiping at the wolves he didn't recognize as pack. He slashed a grey wolf across the belly and moved on to the next. A silverback leaped on him and he sank his teeth into its throat and jerked until the neck snapped. He tossed aside the limp body and shouldered his way through a small band of red wolves that were trying to corner him. He found Michael being double-teamed by a large black wolf with a white streak and a gray wolf with blood pouring from a wound in his side that Rafe's brother must have delivered.

He snarled and leapt onto the injured wolf's back. He

sank his claws deep until the wolf buckled and then used his fangs to rip him apart. The black and white wolf snarled but instead of leaping to the defense of his fallen friend he turned and ran.

Michael was on the ground and Rafe nuzzled him, checking for signs of how hurt he was. It was merely a flesh wound. Michael was okay. He was going to live. He was going to survive. Rafe wasn't going to lose him. Not here and now. Not tonight. Rafe whined and Michael nuzzled him in return, reassuring him that he was okay.

A wolf howled a sound that could only be retreat and the foreign wolves that were still standing began to scatter. Rafe caught sight of the black and white wolf snarling from the woods as his friends raced past him and his own wolf snarled in return. He didn't like that at all. He didn't like that this wolf seemed to be the leader of them and that he'd gone straight for Michael.

His wolf took off after him.

Somewhere behind him, dimly, he heard Michael growl. He knew his brother wanted him to stop. He knew that he should go back and protect his injured little brother. His pack. He should stay but he couldn't stop. He couldn't go back.

He was too close to the edge. He'd lost control and he couldn't get his wolf back in line. He'd known that shifting tonight would have consequences. He'd worried about what would happen but he hadn't worried about this. About losing Michael. And it had pushed him over the edge, not to it but over it.

His human side had burrowed too deep and he wasn't ready to surface yet. His wolf was too powerful. He was crazed with blood lust and terror. The last time this had happened it had taken days for him to regain his skin and years until he felt like he was truly back in control. This time, he wasn't sure he would ever be able to come back.

And this time he really would lose everything.

CHAPTER 23

*Z*oey's heart was racing too fast. So fast, too fast, she thought it might explode. All she could hear was her blood pounding in her ears. All she could feel was the distance between her and her mate growing and it was making her wolf go crazy. She wanted to race after him but the panic inside of her had stopped her in her tracks as soon as she stumbled into the meadow full of fighting wolves.

Fighting wolves. Wolves attacking each other. Teeth and claws and fighting the likes of which she'd never even imagined in her wildest dreams. As soon as she'd seen the battle raging she'd come to a grinding halt as her wolf tried to process what was happening and figure out who was who.

Who was friendly? Who was enemy? Who was pack? Her pack.

Something had happened when she broke through the woods into the clearing. She didn't know what it was. She didn't know how it had happened. But Rafe wasn't the only wolf she could sense anymore. She could identify others within the pack now. She could scent their blood and recognized it as her own. Pack. They were part of her pack.

In the back of her mind, her human side pondered the revelation. Pack. Michael had said she wasn't one of his wolves but she could sense them now. It was like she'd been wearing blinders all night but at the scent of blood, the sight of her friends and family fighting, they'd been ripped away.

She was pack. Moirae pack. That meant Rafe was pack too but...

Zoey's wolf whined and shook her head. Rafe was too far away. She couldn't feel her mate. All she could feel now was the giant hole in her chest that his absence had left behind. She felt empty and lost.

He'd left her. He'd really left her. On her first full moon, during her first shift, he'd left her alone.

Not just alone but unprotected amidst an attack.

Her wolf howled and scuffed at the dirt and Zoey tried to take a few deep breaths and calm her other half down. She needed to focus. She needed to concentrate and take control of the situation. Her human half understood that something terrible had happened here and it had fractured Rafe's tenuous hold on his control. Her wolf only felt his abandonment and she was fluctuating between going after him to rip into him and dismissing him completely.

Zoey tried to push to the surface. She needed to shift. She needed to be human. This was something she needed to handle calmly and rationally. As a human. Her wolf was an animal and she didn't understand how to process this situation through the filters of the past and circumstance and love. Zoey tried again to push to the surface but nothing happened.

Her wolf was too strong. Newborn and fierce, she wasn't giving her skin up easily. She'd gotten through the first few awkward minutes quickly. She'd found her footing in the real world easily and she didn't want to go back inside Zoey so soon. The moon was still up and tonight was hers. Zoey could feel her fighting to stay in control and she didn't know how to convince her other half to give it up.

This was why she needed Rafe. He was supposed to walk her through how to shift back to her human form. He was supposed to be there with her every step of the way. He'd taught her how to let her wolf free but he hadn't shown her how to get herself back out and into her own skin. He was supposed to be here for this.

Panic flooded through her system and her wolf howled again.

"Zo?" Her wolf hissed at the sound of her name and spun to face the person that was slowly moving towards her.

Michael. Her human side surged for the surface but her wolf growled and shook her off. The wolf narrowed her eyes and bared her teeth. Subconsciously she knew that the half-naked man was a friend. She recognized him but she didn't like that he'd gotten so close without her noticing and she didn't like that he smelled similar to her mate, but wasn't him.

"Zoey..." Michael stopped moving towards her and held a hand out, "Zo, it's me. It's Michael. You know me. Calm down."

The wolf tilted her head but didn't move.

"Come on, Zoey." He kept his voice soft and calm, "I know you're in there. Look at me. You need to calm down and shift back so I can talk to you, okay?"

Internally, she rolled her eyes and externally her wolf must have made some sort of similar response because Michael smirked a little. She wanted to yell at him. She wanted to tell him that she was trying to shift back but she didn't know how. But they couldn't talk because she was still a wolf.

"Shit." Michael ran a hand through his hair, "Fucking Rafe. He didn't tell you how, did he?"

Her wolf bared her teeth again and Michael winced.

"Sorry. Sorry. Not insulting your mate." He held both hands up now, "I want to help you find him but first I need you to shift for me. I can't leave you like this. Okay, Zo? So... shift for me, please?"

Zoey tried. She really tried. She reached for the surface with every ounce of willpower she had but her wolf wasn't having any of it. She shook Zoey off and gave an internal growl that was threatening and a little bit scary. Zoey recoiled from the anger her wolf directed at her and felt her panic spike again.

What if her wolf never let her surface again? What if she was too strong? What if this scarred her wolf the way Rafe's was scarred and they were never able to live in harmony again? What if....

"Zoey." Michael's voice had turned hard and her wolf stiffened this time.

There was something different in his tone. Something that made her wolf perk her ears up. She calmed just a hair and twitched as if suddenly uncertain of who she was dealing with.

"That's what I thought..." Michael's brows furrowed slightly and he shook his head, "Son of a bitch, I was wrong. I don't know how it's possible or what changed but... you're one of mine now. You and Rafe both."

Mine. Zoey would've laughed if she'd been in her human skin. How long had she yearned for Michael to call her that? For as long as she could remember she'd wanted to be his. Now her wolf hummed a low growl in her throat.

She wasn't Michael's anything. She belonged with Rafe. He was her mate.

"Jesus, Zo." Michael muttered, "Take it easy. I told you I accept Rafe's claim on you. I get it. You're not... mine... you're just, pack. You're pack and I'm Pack Alpha. Do you know what that means? Can you understand me? Because I need you to understand me before I do what I have to do here."

Zoey swallowed the knot in her throat as she processed past her wolf's line of thinking. Pack. Just like she'd thought when she entered the clearing. She was pack. Moirae pack. She just hadn't thought it through to the logical conclusion. That made Michael her Alpha.

Not Rafe.

Her mind whirled as she tried to figure out the rest of Michael's statement. What did he have to do? She knew that tone of voice, even through the fog of her wolf's simpler mind. She knew that something was going to happen, she just didn't know what and her wolf backpedaled suspiciously.

"Stop." Michael's voice held that deep undercurrent again and this time, she registered it for what it was even as her wolf froze in her tracks.

Power. It flowed out of Michael's throat like a voice unto itself. It coasted over her fur and sank into her skin. It rolled through her veins and she struggled on instinct. She tried to move, tried to back further away from him but her limbs didn't work and the harder she tried to pull, the stronger the hold on her became.

"Easy now." Michael softened and stepped forward again, holding his hands out in a way meant to keep her calm, "Easy Zoey."

He was coming at her like she was an animal that would

spook if he moved too quickly. Which, she supposed she was. Her wolf whimpered but stopped struggling against the hold that Michael's voice had put on her. Then it hit her.

He'd used his Alpha voice on her. Oh, oh, she'd only thought she recognized his power over the pack before, when she'd been human. She hadn't. She really, really hadn't. She hadn't known he could do this. Control a member of the pack through nothing but a demand. And he'd used it on her.

She bared her teeth at him and Michael chuckled, "There's the Zoey I know. That's it. You just figured it out didn't you? What I meant when I said you're mine? You figured out I can make you do anything just by saying it and that pisses you off, doesn't it?"

Her wolf growled.

"Yeah, that's it Zo. Get mad at me. That's fine. You want it to stop? Shift. Shift back for me so I don't have to make you."

Make her. Shift. Zoey struggled for the surface again. Panic was hitting her hard. He could make her shift. That brought back memories of the first shift in the woods. It had hurt so much and she'd wanted it. How much worse would it be if she fought it? She had a feeling her wolf was going to fight it and it was going to be pure agony.

"Yeah." Michael dropped to his heels and his voice dropped into a whisper, "Don't make me do this, Zo. Please. Don't make me hurt you. You know I can't stand seeing you in pain."

Her wolf whined. She whimpered from inside her own skin. She was struggling, trying to break to the surface but she didn't know how. Damnit she didn't know how! She wanted to come back. She needed to come back.

She needed to find Rafe and get him back. But she couldn't find a way to claw her way back to the surface and her wolf was too panicked and agitated to give up control.

Michael sighed heavily, "We're wasting time. I need to be checking on the rest of the pack. I need to figure out what happened and who did it. I need to go after Rafe. But you and I both know before I can deal with any of that I have to take care of you."

Her wolf whimpered.

"You're family, Zo. I have to take care of you." Michael started to reach out, as if he was going to stroke her fur but then seemed to think better of it and pulled his hand back, "Are you ready?" His brows knit together and he closed his eyes, his voice had dropped back into that powerful baritone, "Shift, Zoey. Now. Shift."

The words hit her like a punch to the gut and her wolf hissed. Zoey screamed as her bones cracked and her muscles seized. It was agony. Pure agony as her wolf howled and her throat went raw with the sound of her screams. She doubled over, panting and sweating and the world went fuzzy and then completely black.

"Zoey?" Michael's voice roused her back into consciousness and her eyes flickered open, the world coming back into focus.

She was on the ground, curled up in the fetal position. Everything hurt. Literally everything, even her teeth hurt. She thought she might puke so she pulled air in and out of her lungs slowly. Trying to steady herself and find her equilibrium. Her body was wracked with pains and she moaned as she tried to sit upright.

"Easy, now." This time Michael's hands closed around her upper arms, guiding her into a sitting position and she winced at his strength, "Sorry. Sorry. I know it hurts. I'm sorry."

"Rafe..." Her voice came out a harsh croak and she met Michael's eyes, "We have to find Rafe."

"Zo..." Michael scrubbed a hand over his face but she reached out and grabbed his wrist, pulling his hand away and forcing him to look at her.

"He's hurting. He's scared and alone and..." Her voice broke and she didn't even realize she was crying until Michael softly brushed the stray tears off her cheeks, "Michael, please..."

"I'll get him back for you, Zoey. I promise I will. Just let me take care of you first."

"No." She tried to shove up to her feet to go after her mate herself but her legs were too weak to hold her weight and Michael had to catch her.

"Goddamnit Zoey. You never listen to me." He swept her up into his arms and she became instantly and embarrassingly aware that she was naked.

Naked as the day she was born. In front of the entire pack. Her skin against Michael's as he carried her. And it felt wrong, so wrong. She shivered and tried to cover herself but Michael only chuckled.

"Don't bother. I'm not looking and even if I did, it wouldn't be anything I wanted to see."

She sniffed, "Gee, thanks buddy."

His grin was sparkling when he laughed, "You're my brother's mate. My sister by fate. You're also a member of my pack. You're going to have to get used to the nudity thing if you're going to shift with us going forward. This is nothing."

"You think your brother is going to see it that way?"

Michael's smile faltered. Her chest ached and her wolf

whined from her new place deep inside Zoey. His brother. Her mate. Rafe. She felt incomplete without him. Like her heart was missing from her chest.

"He didn't want to change, Michael." She whispered softly, "He was worried. He was... scared. He didn't know how his wolf would react to me but all of this... the fighting and the blood? It was too much. I can feel him and he's so far away and he's panicked. I need to go after him."

"You're not going anywhere except inside to rest and heal from your first shift. I'm Pack Alpha and whatever happened tonight, it brought him back to me. He's pack again and I can feel him too. I promised you I'd get him back and I will. You have to trust me, Zoey."

"I do. I trust you. And I'll stay here." She met Michael's eyes, the ones that looked so much like her mates, "Find him and bring him back to me."

CHAPTER 24

The sun was coming up but Rafe was still in his wolf form. He hadn't even tried to change back to his human self. He didn't want to be in his skin right now. He didn't feel solid or safe. He'd burrowed down deep inside the animal when he realized he couldn't regain control and he'd let the wolf have his way ever since.

Sadly, his broken wolf had retreated even further than his human side.

The wolf had gone back to their old camping site. The one that they'd stayed at when he was just a pup. The campground that the humans had stumbled upon because it was just outside the pack boundary.

He'd gone back to the place where his family had been slaughtered. The last place he could remember being truly happy. Before his parents and brother were killed and he'd ripped apart two men in his half-crazed bloodlust.

He'd become a killer that day and he'd spent hours, days, out here in the woods wandering around lost and confused. His fur had been soaked in blood and he'd kept going back to the bodies of his family. Here, in these trees and on this ground, he'd mourned all alone, feeling as if he had lost his grip on reality.

Maybe that was why his wolf had come back here last night. He'd lost control. His wolf had taken over. He'd gone murderous at the thought of Michael being injured, being killed. He'd chased those wolves that attacked his brother down. He'd managed to catch a few and he'd ripped them apart just like he had those hunters years ago.

Then he'd come here and lay down, hunkered down, but he hadn't slept a wink. He'd just stared into the woods, waiting for someone to come for him. He'd thought that big wolf might come back for him and try to take him down for what he'd done to his friends. But it had been quiet all night which was why the sound of a twig breaking had him scrambling up.

He jumped into a defensive position and snarled in the direction the noise had come from. His eyes scanned the woods but he couldn't see anything. He growled a warning but it cut off as soon as his brother stepped out from behind a tree.

Michael. Brother. Family. Pack.

His wolf was still jumpy. He didn't know whether to rush Michael and nuzzle him, make sure he was okay, or run away. Michael had shifted back to human before coming to find him. He looked leery but also determined and if the vibes rolling off of him were any indication, he was also frustrated as hell.

Rafe's wolf whined as Michael inched closer.

"Easy now." His brother spoke softly, "Easy, Rafe. I'm not here to hurt you or fight with you. I'm here to bring you home."

Home. Rafe's wolf tilted his head at that. He hadn't had a home in so long.

Michael reached a fallen log and sat on it. He didn't move quickly. He kept his every action slow and steady and his eyes on Rafe's. He didn't get too close. He sat down like he was getting comfortable for a chat and that was Rafe's first sign that they were about to have a very one-sided conversation.

He couldn't talk back in wolf form. Maybe that's what Michael wanted. Hell, maybe it was what he wanted. Because he didn't try to shift back. He simply stared at his brother through his wolf's eyes and waited for him to get to the point.

Dressed as he was in jeans and a t-shirt, Michael looked no worse for wear after the battle last night. He'd healed fast. The only visible sign of any trouble at all was the red mark that ran along his forearm. He'd been cut deep there by a claw at some point during the fighting and it was going to scar.

Rafe's wolf whined as he remembered the panic he'd felt when he heard Michael howl. The sight of his brother on the ground with wolves coming after him had Rafe gritting his teeth. The fact that he could still taste the blood of those wolves, could smell it on his fur, kept him from losing his grip on reality again.

He'd taken care of them and Michael was safe.

"You know I was wrong right?" His brother scrubbed a hand through his hair and shrugged, "Sure you do. You can feel it just like I can. I was wrong about you not being pack anymore. You are. You're Moirae pack. Your tie just isn't to the land. It's to me."

Rafe's wolf eased back down and watched Michael through suspicious eyes. His wolf knew that just like he did. It wasn't news. He'd felt it last night. He didn't know why the bond had needed to be reformed but it was clear that it had. It had taken Michael's blood to do it. Michael had spilled his blood and Rafe had instantly sensed it.

Pack. Family. Brotherhood. He was Moirae.

"Right. You know that." Michael continued, "So you know that if I really wanted to, I could force you to shift back right here and right now."

Rafe's wolf growled. Oh, he didn't like that. He didn't like the threat. He didn't like the reminder that Michael was Pack Alpha. He definitely didn't like the certainty in his little brother's voice that said he knew he was strong enough to do it. In a battle of wills, Michael believed he would win as the Pack Alpha and the only thing that kept Rafe from challenging him in that moment was the knowledge that he would have to be the one to spill more of Michael's blood to prove it untrue.

And he would never do that.

"I'm not going to." Michael shook his head, "Because I have some things I want to say and honestly, I kind of like the idea of you not being able to interrupt me."

Rafe bristled but settled back down. He wasn't going to fight his brother. Not as wolves and not as humans either. Just so long as Michael didn't play the trump card and try to force a change on him that he wasn't ready for.

"I never blamed you, ya know." His brother leaned forward with a heavy sigh and rested his elbows on his thighs, "Never. I always knew what happened to Mom and Dad, what happened to Gabe, wasn't your fault. I've never had a chance to tell you that because you were so busy blaming yourself but I want you to know that I never did."

His wolf whined at the mention of his twin and their parents. It had been his fault. No matter what Michael said. It had been his fault. He hadn't done it on purpose and he would take it back if he could but it was his fault they'd all been in the woods that day and he was the one that had accidentally led the hunters back to their camp. It was his fault their family was dead.

"No. Don't you do that." Michael's voice rose a little, "Don't you get lost back there in the could have's and should have's. It was a long time ago and it's over. Whatever you did that makes you think you caused their deaths, you've more than paid for it with your self-imposed banishment and isolation."

Michael dropped his eyes and picked at a string on the knee of his ripped jeans, "I never blamed you for their deaths but leaving? That was all your choice, Rafe. You left. Left the pack. Left me. Your only family. Your only brother. You left me all alone to deal with everything and I blamed you for that for a long time. I hated you for it."

Rafe felt the words sink into his soul and his wolf whined again. Michael hated him. He'd always secretly wondered if his brother despised him for what had happened in the woods that day. Hearing that he didn't blame him for their family being killed was unexpected but hearing that he hated him wasn't. It just hadn't been for the reason he thought it was.

"The thing is, as I got older and I took on more and more of the pack responsibilities I understood why you left. You were in no shape to lead and you thought leaving was the only way to protect me. It was the only way to give me the pack without the elders stripping you of your Alpha status or making me fight you for it." Michael met his eyes again and a sad smile tilted one corner of his lips, "Yeah. I get that now, brother. I get why you had to leave me behind the way you did and I forgive you."

If he was in his human form, Rafe thought he might have cried. Forgiveness. It was the very last thing he deserved but he wanted it. He soaked in it. His brother forgave him because he was a better man than Rafe had ever been. A better wolf and a better leader. Michael was the Alpha the pack deserved.

"Look at me." Michael's strong, demanding voice jerked Rafe out of his thoughts and he met eyes that had gone hard and golden in the morning light, "I forgive you for leaving me behind but I will never, ever, forgive you if you do the same thing to Zoey."

Zoey. Rafe snapped to attention at the sound of her name. Zoey. His Zoey. His mate. His wolf whined and shrank down into a crouch. He'd forgotten about her. In his bloodlust, he'd somehow forgotten about his mate and that was... unacceptable. Totally and completely unacceptable. His gut clenched and his fur rolled as his wolf tried to scramble away from the accusation.

It was true though. He'd left Zoey. He'd left her in the middle of a battle on her first full moon. He'd left his mate alone without even looking back. In the old days, he'd have been stripped of his wolf for putting a female in danger like that.

He whimpered at the thought of losing her. He could have lost her. He'd only been thinking of Michael All this time and all these hours, he'd been wandering around in a cloud of sorrow for all he'd lost. He'd forgotten somehow of all he had left to lose.

Zoey. The woman he was in love with. His woman and his wolf to cherish and protect and on day one, night one, he'd failed.

"You swore to me that you'd do right by her. You promised you'd be better. So you come home with me now, you come back and you make things right with her. I'm not giving you another option. I wouldn't have fought you for the pack but I'll fight you for her. Not because I want her as my mate but because she's my best friend. She's the best woman I've ever known and I think she's good for you. But you have to be good for her in return."

Rafe was already surging for the surface before his brother finished speaking. His wolf didn't fight him. He let go of his control of them and let Rafe come back to the forefront. He hadn't liked the truth of what he'd done and he didn't want to face off with Michael. His wolf all but tucked tail and ran as Rafe shifted back into his human form.

Michael tilted his head when he was lying on his back, panting, completely naked, "There you are. I figured threatening to fight you for Zo might bring you back around."

"Not fighting you for her." Rafe sucked in a gulp of air through his teeth and narrowed his eyes on his not so little brother, "She's mine."

"Yeah?" Michael raised an eyebrow. "Prove it. Come home with me and do right by her. She's your mate. She's supposed to come first. Even before me, brother."

Rafe lowered his eyes, "I saw you laying there, bloody and hurt and I..."

"I know, but it doesn't matter now. We can deal with that. We can talk pack politics and going after the ones that came onto our land. We'll figure out how to coexist as two Moirae Alphas on pack land. We're family and we can figure all of that out later. Right now, Zoey comes first."

"From now on." Rafe nodded his agreement, "From now on she comes first. I'll do better. I swear I will."

"I'm going to hold you to that."

"Good. I'm glad we finally agree on something."

Michael chuckled and pushed up from the log he'd been sitting on, "Brought you some clothes, I don't really want to walk all the way back to the lodge pretending you're not balling out."

Rafe smiled. He smiled and it felt like for the first time, his heart was full of hope again. Love, again. He loved his brother and he loved Zoey. He just had to hope that when he got back to town that the damage he had done wasn't irreparable. He had to hope that she loved him enough to forgive him.

And hope was a strangely foreign emotion.

CHAPTER 25

Zoey could actually see the path in the grass that she'd worn down from all her pacing. Michael had left her hours ago to go looking for Rafe. She'd tried to go with him but he'd ordered her to stay put.

Ordered!

Michael had given her an order and as her Alpha, she had to follow it. Which pissed her off to no end. Whenever he showed his stupid, arrogant, bossy ass back up she was going to give him a piece of her mind. She'd been his best friend far longer than she'd been a member of his pack.

And Rafe was her mate. Hers. Sure he was Michael's brother but mate trumped brother.

She rubbed her hands up and down her arms as she paced. She should be out there. Looking for Rafe. Tracking him down. Finding her mate and making sure he was okay so that she could rip him apart herself for going off alone during an attack.

Jesus, Zoey swallowed hard around the knot in her throat.

They'd been attacked. Another pack had come onto

Moirae land and injured members of the pack. They'd gone after Michael. Taken him down. Tried to take him out. It had been a measured and deliberate act of violence. They'd wanted to kill Michael. They could have. And even though he was out there in the woods, walking around, a new scar on his arm and only a few bruises to show thanks to his superhuman genes, she couldn't shake the thought of how close she'd come to losing him.

How close she'd come to losing them both.

She loved them. Both of them. She loved Michael as her best friend, as the brother she'd sworn she never would. She loved him with the pure, undiluted innocence of the girl she'd been. And she loved Rafe as her mate and her lover, her fate and her destiny. She loved him with her whole heart and soul, her entire being and two sides of her self. She loved them and she'd almost lost them.

Her wolf whined and clawed at her insides. She didn't want to think about that. She wanted to be out there, in the woods, on their scent. She wanted to find the wolves that had attacked her family and rip them to shreds. And she only consoled herself that she would, once she knew her men were safe.

"Zoey, why don't you..."

She whirled at the sound of her name and hissed, "So help me Darius if you tell me I should go inside and relax I'm going to claw your eyes out."

The Enforcer didn't even flinch from his position on the steps of the lodge where he'd been standing the entire time she paced. His lips turned down at the corners even more than usual, something she hadn't known was possible. He always looked annoyed and disapproving but this time she didn't take it personally.

Darius had been as pissed as she was when Michael

told him to stay like a good little lapdog too. He wasn't the type to openly argue with his Pack Alpha which was why the fact that he'd questioned the logic of Michael going out alone after an attack had been brow raising. Michael had said he would be fine and for Darius to stay with Zoey and the others in the pack who were still recovering from their injuries. Darius hadn't once gone inside to check on the others. He'd stayed on the porch and intermittently watched the woods and watched her pace and each time he'd opened his stupid mouth it had been to tell her she should go inside and get some rest.

On a normal day, she wanted to smack him for being a condescending, arrogant ass. Today? She really wanted to unleash her new claws on his stone-cold face.

When he remained silent she sniffed and went back to pacing. She was surrounded by stupid, know-it-all men that thought they could tell her what to do. Well screw that. Michael was getting a serious talking to when he got back and so was Rafe. Darius wasn't the real source of her outrage anyway. He might think a woman's place was to stand silent and sweetly behind her male but that wasn't Zoey. It never had been and she wasn't about to start now when she finally had the power of a wolf inside of her. She could and would defend herself and her mate if need be. She wouldn't be left behind again.

When Rafe came back she was going to...

"Rafe." Her head jerked up as every single one of her senses began to tingle. Her wolf clawed at her again, wanting out, but she shook off the urge to shift. He was close and her eyes darted over the tree line, looking, looking... "Rafe."

She was running before his name ever left her lips. Her brain had only barely registered his presence as he stepped from between the trees. His hair was disheveled and his five o'clock shadow had turned into a beard. His chest was bare and there were thin red lines that looked like healing scratches. The jeans he wore hung low on his hips and he was barefoot.

He'd never looked better to her.

"Rafe." She flew into his arms and he caught her with a grunt. His big arms went around her, squeezing her tight and holding her close. He dipped his head, nuzzling against her hair and she clung to him with every fiber of her being, "Oh God, I thought..."

"I'm sorry." Rafe murmured softly, "I'm so sorry, baby."

Zoey held onto him for a moment longer. She let her wolf nuzzle up against her skin to get close to him. She felt his wolf do the same. Their breathing synched and they clung to each other. Her nerves began to settle now that he was here. He was safe and he was in one piece. He wasn't hurt.

"Don't you ever do that to me again!" She shoved out of his arms and stumbled when she broke free.

Rafe winced and his eyes lowered, "I'm sorry."

"Not good enough."

"I, uh... I'll leave you two alone." Michael cleared his throat and when she glanced at him, realizing he was at Rafe's side for the first time he smiled softly, "Hear him out, Zo."

"Oh, he's not the only one I'm angry at." She glared at her best friend, "I get you're more than my best friend now. You're my Alpha and that means you're in charge. But you can't order me to let my mate go ever again. Do you hear me, Michael? It's not fair."

"Being a wolf isn't always fair, Zo. But you know I'm only ever looking out for you, it's all I've ever done."

"I know that." She conceded.

"I was just trying to..."

"Finish that sentence with *protect me* and I might actually hit you, Alpha or not."

Michael snorted at her idle threat and gave his older brother a big pat on the shoulder, "She's all yours now, bro. Good luck."

She glared at her oldest friend in the world as he smirked and walked away. She stuck her tongue out at him behind his back and even though he couldn't see it, Darius could. To her utter amazement, she thought she saw a flicker of a smile cross the Enforcer's face before he too lowered his gaze. She turned back to her mate, the true source of her irritation, and he was smart enough not to be smiling.

She studied him for a moment and some of her anger lost its steam. Yes, he was here and he seemed unhurt but he wasn't okay. His eyes were dark and haunted and her heart ached. All she wanted was to hug him close and never let him go again but she knew she couldn't cuddle this problem away.

"We need to talk."

"Actually," Rafe glanced up from beneath his dark lashes, "I need to talk, to you. Could you maybe just... hear me out?"

"I'm waiting." She nodded.

Rafe shifted from one foot to another. He twisted his hands together and then dropped them to his sides. When he glanced back up at her, he looked absolutely stricken and it took her a moment to realize what the emotion on his handsome face was.

Guilt.

"Rafe?"

"I uh... there's something I need to tell you." Rafe took a deep breath and didn't meet her eyes when he spoke again, "Last night, when I turned with you... Zo. Baby. That was the first time I've fully turned since I lost Gabe and my parents."

Zoey sucked in a gulp of air as his admission hit her right in the gut. It had been... years and years. Months and months of full moons and Rafe was a full-blooded, born Alpha wolf. Yet he hadn't changed? He was telling her that he hadn't shifted, that he'd somehow resisted his wolf's urges and needs all this time.

No wonder his wolf had freaked out.

"Are you kidding me?" She gaped at him.

"Zo..."

"You haven't shifted in years and you didn't think that was pertinent information that I should have known?"

"I know. I should have told you. I'm sorry."

"How? Why? I mean... that's why you were so worried about letting him near me, right? That's why you were scared of claiming me? Marking me? You should have told me why."

"I know. I just thought..." Rafe ran a hand through his hair, "I didn't want you to worry."

Zoey pinched the bridge of her nose and closed her eyes. She took a deep breath and then let it out slowly. She knew that admitting this to her was hard for him. She didn't want to make it harder. She didn't want to push him away. But this was all so new to her. She'd been around the pack her entire life and she'd thought she had a place in it but until Rafe came back, she hadn't been a wolf and there was still so much she had to learn. Rafe keeping things from her, even if it was in a bid to protect her, wasn't the way for her to find her new place within this pack.

She opened her eyes again and stared up at a devastated looking Rafe when she shook her head, "I can't do this."

"Zoey, no, please..." He reached for her and she sighed.

"I'm not walking away from you, Rafe." She stepped closer to him again to reinforce her words, "I can't. I wouldn't even know how. You're my mate. You're my other half. I don't want to leave you but I don't want to lose you either."

"You won't."

"I could have and all because you thought you were protecting me by keeping me in the dark." She argued. "Last night, you disappeared. You let your wolf take over and he bolted." She held her hand up when he started to speak again, "I get that he was scared. I know you were scared. I was scared too though. It was my first full moon. My first shift. And my mate abandoned me in the middle of a war zone. Do you have any idea how terrified I was?"

Rafe winced.

"I didn't even know how to shift back. You were supposed to help me with that, remember? You weren't there and my wolf was scared to death. I couldn't control my emotions enough to shift back on my own. Did Michael tell you that?" She tilted her head when he didn't meet her eyes, "Did he tell you that he had to force me to shift back?"

"Fuck. Zoey." Rafe's voice was hoarse with emotions, "I'm so sorry. I fucked up. I know. I know sorry doesn't cover it, not even close, but I can promise you that it will never happen again."

"Damn right it's not going to happen again." She tilted his chin so that he had to look her in the eyes, "Because you're not going to keep secrets from me anymore. Do you understand? I won't stand for it. I'm your mate, not your pup. I don't need you to protect me from the truth. We're partners. Equal partners from here on out."

"I promise." Rafe pulled her into his arms again and hugged her tight, "I promise, Zoey. I won't hurt you again. You come first. I swear. I fucked up but now you know, you got stuck with a defective wolf, a defective mate. Michael was right, I'm not stable and I'm not good enough for you but I'm your mate and you're mine and I'll be better. I promise."

Zoey gripped him tighter as his words sank in, "You're not defective. Don't you ever say that again."

"I'm a mess."

"You're my mess." She nuzzled against his chest.

"I'm so sorry. I'll make it up to you, I swear."

"Just promise me that you won't leave me like that again. I don't want to lose you, Rafe. Not when I just found you. Not when we have our whole lives together ahead of us."

"I'm not going anywhere. I promise."

"Me either."

"Except home." He amended as he pulled back and cupped her cheeks, "Can we go home?"

Zoey's eyes watered a bit at the question. Home. He wanted to go home. He was standing on pack land just outside the lodge his parents had owned, but that wasn't what he was talking about. He wanted to go home, to the cabin, with her. And he was right. It already felt more like home than her apartment ever had. Because it was theirs.

"Yeah." She tiptoed up and kissed him softly, "Let's go home."

CHAPTER 26

Rafe held tight to Zoey's hand as she led him up the steps of their cabin. Michael had graciously lent them one of the pack vehicles to get home and they'd driven in silence. It hadn't been the most comfortable silence they'd shared but he'd known they both had a lot to think about. It had been a long night, a scary night, but they were still together and that was what mattered.

He followed Zoey through the door into the cabin and shut it behind them. The smell of them was everywhere. All of their hours of lovemaking from the day before, of their mating, it permeated the air and filled his lungs. It made his wolf rouse from his slumber and brush at his insides. When Zoey started to let go of his hand, he held tight and pulled her close instead.

"Rafe?"

He tugged her against his body, holding her in a tight hug and she accepted easily. She wound her arms around him as well and they stood there like that for a long time. Intertwined. Breathing the same air. Their hearts synching as they fell into one another and he felt that now familiar ache in his chest whenever he thought of losing her.

He was an idiot. He'd been trying to hold back and go slow, for her. But Zoey had never asked him for that. She'd rushed headlong into this relationship, accepting that fate had a plan and accepting him as her mate. He'd been stupid keeping secrets from her and he swore that he would never do it again as he breathed in her warm, sweet scent until it permeated his blood.

"Zo?" He brushed her hair back and leaned away enough to look down at her beautiful face, "There's something else I need to tell you."

Her brows pinched slightly but she didn't pull away, "What is it?"

"Last night, when we sealed the bond and mated fully, it was your first change and a full moon and..."

A small smile tugged at Zoey's lips, "Are you trying to tell me I might be pregnant?"

His eyebrows hit his hairline, "You know?"

"I grew up with the pack." Zoey nodded, "I know how it works even if I didn't have my own wolf until now. I know pregnancies are high after a full moon, particularly for the young in the pack that have undergone the change recently and are mated. So yeah, I know."

Rafe rubbed his thumb over her cheekbone, "And you're okay with that?"

"Of course I'm okay with that. I'm more than okay with it. Rafe, you're my mate. I want us to have a family together. I want us to have everything we've both ever dreamed of."

His heart ached again at the strength of his tiny little mate. She was gorgeous inside and out. Beautiful and sweet and kind and understanding, he'd done nothing in his life to deserve her but he would. He thought maybe that was why the fates had seen fit to gift him with her as his other half. She made him want to be better.

"You're everything I ever dreamed of, Zoey."

She cuddled her cheek into his touch, "Are you worried I might be pregnant?"

"Only about you. Carrying pups, I've heard it's difficult and I don't want you to hurt, not for a second."

"I can handle it."

"I know. I just worry." He dropped his forehead to hers and lowered his voice, "I don't want to lose you."

"You won't." Zoey covered his hands with her own and held him close. "You won't."

Rafe brushed his lips over hers and groaned when she sighed a sound of contentment that rocked him. He did it again, loving that sound. And again, and again, until her sighs had turned from content to something else. Needy. He pressed his mouth to hers harder and when she tiptoed up, trying to keep him close he groaned as he broke away and hauled her up into his arms.

"I love the sounds you make when I touch you."

Zoey wrapped herself around him, a glint in her eyes, "I love when you touch me."

"I need you, baby." He nipped at her jaw, "Let me make love to you. No heat forcing it on us. No wolves clawing for each other. Just you and me. You're my mate, Zo. You're my woman. My other half. You make me whole." He pulled back again just enough to meet her eyes, wanting to see her when he admitted a truth that seemed as natural as breathing, "I love you."

Zoey's bottom lip trembled slightly and she bit into it, steadying herself. Tears glistened in her eyes but she blinked them away. Her answering smile eased some of the tension the tears had caused to ratchet up in his chest and she soothed him completely when she nodded.

"I love you too, Rafe."

"You do?"

"Of course I do." She brushed his hair back from his forehead, "You're my mate and my man and my other half. You make me whole too."

The weight that he felt like he'd been carrying around inside of him for years eased a bit at her words. She loved him. He didn't know how or why. He knew he wasn't easy to love. He was half-feral, wild and untamed. He was gruff and rude and add to that he was overbearing and dominant. But she loved him and that made him look at his entire life in a new light.

Everything he'd gone through, it had been to get him here. To her. Maybe if he'd stayed all those years ago he would have known she was his long before now, but he wasn't sure he would have been ready for her then. Just like she hadn't been ready for him. Fate had a plan and this was their part of it. Mates, together, finally.

"Let me love you, Zo."

She was the one that pressed their mouths together and he groaned when she tried to take control. She could be a bossy little thing and he loved that about her. But this, this would always be where his alpha nature refused to give up control. He wrapped a hand in her hair and tugged gently, but enough to sting, causing her to gasp and give him the upper hand.

His tongue was in her mouth a second later and Zoey whimpered and arched against him. Her taste spread through him and his wolf growled, wanting more of their mate. Rafe consciously pushed the animal down, wanting

Zoey for himself as he carried her towards their bedroom. This was about them.

Once he'd kicked the door to the bedroom shut behind them he slowly lowered Zoey to the ground, "Clothes off. Gonna burn this shit and kill my brother if he ever loans you another item of clothing."

Zoey giggled softly and made quick work of tugging off the oversized shirt she'd been wearing, "It was this or go naked at the lodge. I assumed you're prefer the rest of the pack not see me undressed but I guess I can refuse the clothes next time."

A growl worked its way up his throat making her laugh again as he snatched the clothes from her and tossed them aside, "Nobody sees you like this but me."

"Possessive bastard." She teased.

"My mate." He dropped his pants and kicked them off, "Mine. Kill anybody that so much as looks at you."

"You're so sexy when you're acting like a homicidal maniac." Zoey giggled again as she stepped forward and stroked a hand down his chest, "You're mine too, Rafe. Remember that."

"Yours." He groaned as her fingers danced across his hip, "I'm all yours, baby."

"This too." Her voice dropped low as she wrapped her small hand around his rock-hard length and his hips automatically kicked forward. "This is mine."

"Fuck, yes."

"Just in case I'm not knocked up yet, why don't you come here and put a pup in me." She tugged gently, all but leading him by his dick towards the bed and like a dog desperate for her attention he followed. "I want what's mine, mate."

Rafe was on her instantly. He tossed her onto the bed and followed her down, pinning her beneath him. Mate. God, was there a better word in the English language? He loved it. Loved that he was hers. Loved it when she called him hers. Her mate.

He nudged her thighs open and notched himself between them as he took her mouth again. She was all movement beneath him. Arching and rolling her hips, her nails scoring his back as she urged him closer. She was needy, for him, and he loved it. Wanted nothing more than to sate her, to give her what she needed from him, but before he did, he had one more thing he knew they needed to talk about.

He broke the kiss and trailed his lips across her jaw, towards her ear, "Zo, baby, I want you to marry me."

She gasped and he leaned back to look her in the eyes. She was breathing hard and her bottom lip was pinned between her teeth again. Her beautiful eyes searched his face and whatever she found there made her soften, made her hold him tight even as her body stilled beneath him.

"Are you asking?" She finally spoke softly, her throat bobbing as she swallowed hard.

"Yes." He forced out even though they both knew he wanted to make it an order, "Will you marry me, Zoey? You're my mate. You're my heart. I love you more with every breath I take and I can't imagine my life without you. I don't want to. We're already mated, we sealed the bond but I want the ceremony too. I want to tie you to me in every way I can and I want it now."

"Now?" Her lips teased into a smile.

He chuckled at her sense of humor and rocked his hips against her, "Well, not now-now but, before you birth our pups now, for sure." He nuzzled her lips, "I know it's fast but that's how we wolves do things. Fast and completely, we don't do anything in half measure and you're mine. I just want to make it official."

"Okay."

His eyebrows shot up again, "Okay? Okay you'll marry me or..."

"Yes." She giggled and cupped his jaw, "Yes, I'll marry you Rafe. I want you tied to me in every way too. My mate. My husband. My everything."

His eyes burned and he squeezed them shut tight, trying to keep back tears. Everything. She was his everything and she was going to give him everything he'd ever wanted. A home and a family. He had the perfect little mate and she was his, all his.

When he opened his eyes she was stroking his hair gently, caressing and soothing him in the way that only she could and his voice broke, "I love you."

"I love you too." She leaned up and nipped at his lips. "I love you, Rafe."

He kissed her again, hard and possessive, and she wrapped herself around him. Right where she belonged. With him. Against him. He rocked his hips and groaned. Surrounding him. His wolf hummed from deep inside his chest. He was happy and content too for the first time in so long. They were in agreement. Zoey was theirs and they were going to do right by her. They were going to make her happy. Give her world. Because they were hers too.

He slid a hand between them and Zoey gasped and arched, crying out his name, "Rafe!"

"You ready for me, baby?"

"So ready." She whimpered.

He groaned at that answer because he knew it was true. She was wet. Soft, hot, wet heat welcomed him when he pushed his hips forward and he groaned at the feel of her.

Like coming home. He thought it would always feel like that when he was with her. Completion.

"Wrap your legs around me." He groaned as he levered himself up, finding the right angle and driving in hard when she complied. They both gasped. "God you feel so damn good."

"So do you." Zoey scratched his shoulders as she held on, "Harder."

"My mate likes it a little rough?" He bit her shoulder lightly and she shivered beneath him in response. "Yeah, you like making me lose control don't you, baby?"

"Yes." Her hands slid to his ass, pulling him against her as she rocked her hips up into him, "Yes, yes, yes."

"So fucking perfect for me." He groaned as her body clenched and clutched at him, "Love you Zo."

"Love you." She whimpered and one of her hands released him, going to the headboard to hold herself down as his thrusts increased and threatened to send her through the wall, "Oh God, Rafe, just like that."

"Yeah? You close?" He knew she was, could feel it in the way her body tensed, could smell it on her skin, taste it on her lips.

"Yes. Oh God... Rafe, more... I need..." Her breaths were coming in pants and her body was straining, aching for the release he could give her, but he knew she couldn't get there alone. Not like this. He knew what she needed. Knew even if she couldn't ask for it in this state.

He bared his teeth and slammed into her hard and deep as he closed his mouth around his bite mark on her neck. Zoey screamed and her orgasm ripped through her. Rafe closed his eyes and let himself go. He rode it out, feeling her body accept everything he gave it as he pumped and pumped and his cock twitched as he released jet after jet into her welcoming body. He didn't release his bite until the last tremor had rocked through them both and they fell to the bed together, panting and disheveled.

Using his tongue, he licked the bite mark that was already starting to heal thanks to her new shifter abilities. Zoey hummed but didn't open her eyes. She simply wrapped herself around him as if he might try to pull away. He didn't. He let her hold him in the aftermath of their love-making and enjoyed the feel of her, enjoyed knowing that he would get to spend the rest of his life with her like this.

"Mmm." Zoey finally sighed, wiggling against him until she found a comfortable position, her voice sleepy, "If I wasn't pregnant before, I think I definitely am now."

Rafe chuckled softly and hugged her close, "We can keep trying, just to make sure."

Zoey's laughter was his everything, "I'm going to need a few minutes to rest first."

"Sleep, little mate. It's been a long night and something tells me it's going to be a really long day too. Get some rest. I'll be here when you wake."

"You sleep too." She murmured softly, already falling into the clutches of her dreams.

"Okay baby." Rafe kissed the top of her head as he hugged her to his chest.

But he didn't sleep. He couldn't. He had a mate now. A mate that even now was probably growing his pups inside of her. He might never sleep again because he had to keep them safe. Zoey. His family. His brother. His pack. Their safety was his number one priority now that he was back and he wasn't going to sleep until he found that black and white wolf that had attacked them and put him in the ground, once and for all.

CHAPTER 27

Zoey felt every eye in the room turn to her as she walked into the pack lodge. It had been happening her entire life. Ever since she became friends with Michael and began to hang around the pack. Ever since the entire town seemed to figure out that she had feelings for their Pack Alpha that she could do nothing about. They'd been looking at her for years with a mix of pity and suspicion but not anymore.

Today, well today they were looking at her with wide, shocked eyes and she knew why. This was the first time she'd ever been invited to a pack meeting, impromptu or not. This meant she was one of them. But as big as that news was, walking in on the arm of Rafe Hudson was the reason they were all staring.

He'd only been back a few days. Everyone knew about the fight between him and Michael. They knew he'd claimed her as his mate. And they were staring because for the first time in as long as they'd known her she wasn't at Michael's side. Everything had changed and this, walking into the pack headquarters with Rafe at her side, it cemented their bond in a way that she hadn't even realized they needed.

Not just for her either. It also confirmed Rafe's standing in the pack. This wasn't an open meeting. This was for pack higher ups. Michael and his closest circle of advisors and enforcers. Rafe being invited here confirmed that he and Michael were on good terms. There wasn't going to be an Alpha battle to run the pack.

Rafe was a Hudson. He was Moirae. He was an Alpha. But he wasn't going to fight his brother for the pack, which meant there was no need for discourse or mistrust. He could be welcomed back into the fold now. And Michael's smile when he saw them come in together only confirmed it.

Zoey smiled back at him, as much out of habit as out of love. Not the same kind of love she'd had for him before. Not even close. There were no sparks there between her and Michael. Not anymore. Maybe there never had been. Certainly not like the sparks she felt with Rafe. Because as much as she had felt like she and Michael were meant to be, fate had known better.

It was Rafe. It had always been Rafe. They were perfect for each other and she only hoped that someday, maybe even soon, Michael would find the woman that made him whole too. The woman that made him happy. The way that Rafe made her so, so happy.

Her mate, possessive bastard that he was, took one look at the room full of strong, shifter males and tucked her into his side. A low growl bubbled in his throat and she hid a smile against his shoulder. It was crazy but she loved him for his insane urge to keep her for himself, so much so that even having other males look at her annoyed him. She wasn't a big fan of the few women in the room that looked him up and down either so she wound herself around her big, strong, gorgeous mate and let out a hum of content when he squeezed her close.

She loved him. He had been right. It was fast and crazy but she loved him. She was a wolf now and all of her emotions were heightened. She felt everything more strongly than she ever had before, as if the blinders had come off when she'd become a shifter. She loved him with her whole heart and soul, couldn't imagine wanting anyone else or how she'd managed to go so long without him.

Fate had a plan all along. Rafe was right for her in ways that Michael hadn't been, she'd just been too blinded by her devotion to him to see it. Rafe needed her. She was the only one that could put his broken pieces back together. Just like he was the only one that could keep up with her without suffocating her, could support her without her having to take a backseat. He didn't want her to stand behind him. He wanted her right there at his side.

"Rafe. Zoey. Glad you could join us." Michael gave them a nod before motioning to the others, "I'm sure you don't need introductions."

There were a couple of smirks and snorts but everyone nodded. One or two people greeted them with smiles and welcomes. Darius never flinched from his position on Michael's right side. His eyes slid over them but kept going, as if he were searching for threats within the safest space on pack territory.

Zoey didn't understand it. They'd been attacked last night but that had been outdoors and during the full moon. Nobody was stupid enough to lay siege to the Moirae pack lodge during broad daylight. But when Michael spoke again she immediately understood the tension radiating off of the big enforcer.

"As I mentioned before, I've invited a friend to join us

today to discuss last night's attack. Some of you already know him but for those of you that don't, meet Leo DeLuca, rightful heir of the Crescent pack."

A big, dark haired man stood up and went to join Michael at the front. He had dark features. Dark skin and dark hair trimmed short to his scalp. dark eyes that looked bottomless beneath long lashes. He was handsome, more than handsome really, though he didn't compare to Rafe in her opinion. She knew the females must go nuts for him with those looks and the Alpha vibes he radiated. But he looked tired, a little too thin and haggard, as if he hadn't gotten a good nights sleep in weeks, maybe even years.

She wanted to hug him but she figured that would cause more problems for all of them.

Zoey glanced at her mate when she felt him tense beside her but when she looked up she stopped breathing. Rafe was... smiling. Jesus Christ, her ovaries nearly exploded at the sight. Rafe was sexy when he was being broody and overprotective. Smiling? He was downright irresistible. He grinned as he watched his brother and his friend clap hands and hug briefly.

"Did you know about this?" She whispered.

Rafe gave a quick nod, "Michael told me he'd asked Leo to come. I didn't know he'd agreed but I'm not surprised. His family, his pack, is in danger."

Zoey hugged her mate tighter as she remembered what she'd overheard during his conversation with Michael.

The Crescent wolves were their neighboring pack. The DeLuca's had run it for generations. Leo was the eldest son and an Alpha heir but his father had been challenged by a crazy out of control lunatic wolf. His father had been murdered and his sisters had been taken hostage. He needed help to regain his pack and he'd come to the Moirae pack hoping to get it.

It didn't take her long after putting that together to realize why Leo DeLuca was here now.

"The Crescents were behind the attack on our pack last night." Michael announced and then held up a hand when several of the wolves in the room began to snarl in Leo's direction, "This wasn't his doing. We've all heard the rumors. We know that we've received members of the Crescent pack that defected after a new Alpha took charge. Leo's here because he needs help reclaiming his pack before the bastard that killed his father does any more damage."

"Why did he come after us?" One of the other enforcers spoke up from across the room.

"I don't know." Leo admitted when everyone looked to him, "Maybe because he's power hungry and he wants more than just the Crescent land or he found out somehow that I'd asked Rafe to get the Moirae pack involved, to have my back when I challenge him."

"So you brought this on us." Another spoke up and Rafe growled beside her.

"Easy." She squeezed his hand reassuringly but she couldn't help a growl of her own.

She understood why her mate was upset and she agreed with him completely. Leo had come to them for help. He hadn't come here to be further attacked for something that wasn't his fault. He was only trying to save his family.

"Leo didn't bring this fight to our door. It would have come sooner or later. An Alpha like this one, he wants power and he's willing to go to any lengths to get it." Michael spoke up, "I don't know why he came after me in particular but I do know that we're not going to let this stand. We've always had a peaceful relationship with the Crescent pack but we're aligning ourselves with DeLuca now. If you have a problem with that, speak now."

There were a few murmurs but ultimately Michael stared everyone down until they were quiet. His power radiated through the room. There was so much testosterone in the air, Zoey felt like she could choke on it. A room full of Alpha male werewolves was a tense place to be and she knew now why Rafe had wanted her to stay home before ultimately relenting and letting her accompany him to this meeting.

This place was like a powder keg just waiting for a spark to send it up in flames.

"Good." Michael clapped his hands in front of him ,"Now that we're all on the same page, I'll fill you in on the plan."

"Plan?"

"We're going to hit them just as hard as they hit us. No warnings. No attempts at diplomacy. We're gong in hard and fast tomorrow night. The mission is to find and extract the DeLuca girls. There are three of them being held hostage and Leo believes they're in two separate locations so we'll break into two teams. I'll lead one and Darius will lead the other."

"Wait, you're going in?" Rafe growled, pushing to his feet. "You're our Alpha. You should stay here where it's safe. You're still recovering from your injuries as it is."

Michael frowned at his brother, "You're right. I am Pack Alpha. That's why I'm going."

"Michael, I think..." Zoey tried but he held up a hand to quiet her.

"I don't lead from the sidelines. You should know that by now. I'm going."

"Then I'm going too." Rafe used a tone that brooked no argument.

He and Michael had a minor stare down and Zoey held her breath. Would it always be like this? Would they always push each other's buttons? Or would they eventually figure out how to coexist? She didn't dare try to get in between them this time. She knew better now. And after a long minute, Michael nodded.

"Fine."

"Thank you." Rafe lowered his head in acceptance.

Zoey frowned, hating the idea of her mate going into another fight. She'd barely gotten him back this time. If he went into another battle and he lost focus, if he lost his grip or his control, she might lose him for good.

But then Rafe sat back down beside her and pulled her into his lap.

She squeaked, "Rafe!"

"Shh." He nuzzled his face into her hair, "I can feel how much you worry about me, mate. I love you. I love you so much. I'm not ever leaving you again. I have to go to protect Michael and keep him safe. If something happened because I wasn't there... I'd never forgive myself. You have to trust me to get both of us back here to you."

Zoey hugged him tight, amazed all over again at the way he read her so easily. He understood her. He had from the moment their eyes met and the bond had stretched to life between them. She held onto him and reminded herself that he was right. He was a strong, Alpha warrior wolf and he needed to find his place here, in the pack, with his brother. It was the only way he would ever be happy here.

"Okay." She murmured softly. "Just come back to me."

"Always."

Rafe kissed her softly and she returned his kiss. His

hands cupped her waist and slid to her ass. She felt a flare of heat lick through her veins and moaned into his mouth. And then someone cleared their throat loudly and they broke apart with a gasp.

Zoey blushed when she realized everyone was staring at them. Rafe chuckled and cuddled against her. She tried and failed to hide her embarrassment at having forgotten where they were for a moment there.

"As I was saying..." Michael gave them a censorious look but couldn't hide the flicker of amusement in his eyes, "If nobody else has anything to add, we'll break for now and regroup tonight to go over the plan."

"I have something to add." Rafe spoke up and Zoey eyed him like he'd lost his mind.

Michel was letting them go. There was plenty of time left in the day for them to get back to the cabin and have some private time before Rafe went off on this mission tonight. But he was stalling?

"You do?" Michael looked between them expectantly.

"We have a wedding ceremony to plan once we take care of this Crescent situation." Rafe announced loud and clear for everyone in the room to hear.

There were shouts and cheers of celebration at the news. Wolves loved a good party. A wedding ceremony was the best excuse of all. It was the start of a new family within the pack, which increased their strength and numbers. This one would be even more special because it meant Rafe was coming back into the pack and Zoey grinned when Michael smiled at her and mouthed two simple words.

"Thank you."

She nodded at him, wanting to say the same. If it wasn't for him, she wouldn't have stuck around Noir. She might never have known Rafe was her mate. She might never have felt like she belonged here but she did now.

This was home. This was her pack. This was her family.

Michael gave a small bow of acceptance and then turned his attention back to his brother, "It's about time."

Zoey smiled because she knew it was meant as a joke. Rafe had only been in town a couple of days. They'd gone through every phase of their relationship at super-speed. But it wasn't really a joke. It had taken them all a really long time to get here, to this point, to find their way to each other and figure out how they fit together. And now that they had, she couldn't wait to see what fate had in store for them next.

EPILOGUE

LUNA

Something was wrong. The door slamming hard enough to rattle the frame of the small house was the first clue. The sound of scattering footsteps above her was the second. Everyone in the Crescent pack knew to run when their new Alpha was in a mood.

Luna DeLuca knew better than anyone but she couldn't run. He'd made sure of that when he locked her in this damp, musty basement. When he'd chained her with silver. As if her wolf needed to be further weakened.

She was submissive.

One hard word from her Alpha and her wolf cringed and curled up in a ball in defeat. One order and she bent her neck to obey. Her wolf had long since accepted that they were doomed to this sad, pitiful existence and she'd given up trying to fight it.

Even if Luna hadn't.

Her mind wasn't as sharp as it usually was. Being confined, being constrained, it was as good as lodging a dagger in the side of a shifter. It weakened her wolf and that weakened her. She couldn't even remember the last time he let her out to run. She could barely remember what freedom felt like.

Joy. Happiness. Independence. They were long lost memories, faded and dingy at the edges. Some days she wasn't even sure they were memories at all. Some days she thought they were dreams.

This basement was her life now. It had been for weeks, possibly even months. She didn't know because when he'd dragged her here and chained her she hadn't been coherent. She'd been drowning in her grief and her pain. In the loss of her family. He'd forced her to watch while he murdered her father. He'd ripped her family from her and with it a part of her sanity.

She hadn't tried counting the days and nights she'd spent down here. There was no use. Nobody was coming for her. If anyone had cared enough to try and reach her, they'd have done it by now. Either that, or if they had, they'd been stopped. Been put down, murdered and killed just like her father.

Like Leo.

She whimpered at the memory of her brother but shook the awful thought away. Her brother wasn't dead. He wasn't. If he were, she would have known. Somehow, she would have felt it. Because he wasn't just her brother he was her twin, her littermate. Leo was alive. He had to be. But he hadn't come for her.

She'd played through all of the scenarios in her time alone. Leo getting away, running away and starting a new life. But that wasn't her brother. He loved his sisters. He loved this pack. So, was he caught? Captured? Stuck in some other musty basement, chained and weakened by silver? Or was she simply so far gone that her delusions had kept her from accepting the truth, that her brother had been caught and just as brutally murdered as her father had been.

She didn't know. Couldn't be sure. Not about anything. Not anymore.

The lock on the door at the top of the stairs clicked loudly and Luna scuttled back into the dark corner of the room like a frightened mouse. She knew what was coming, or more specifically who. Her tormenter, her captor, the man that had murdered her father and kidnapped her sisters, that had named himself the new Crescent pack Alpha, tread heavy steps as he sauntered down towards her.

He came into view slowly through the dim light. First those thick hiking boots, then dark denim encasing long powerful legs. She closed her eyes at the sight of the deep crimson that could only be blood staining his hands. By the time she worked up the nerve to reopen them, he was on the ground, standing just in front of her and he looked just as angry as she'd imagined he was when she heard him come thundering into the house.

His handsome face, and wasn't it absolutely revolting that she still thought of him as handsome, was twisted into a scowl. His eyes, those intense green eyes that were rimmed in the dark blue of midnight, were cold and mean. She wished she'd noticed that earlier, instead of just their mesmerizing color. Maybe then she could have stopped all of this. His dark beard and hair were both streaked with blood too, as if he'd been running his hands through it. But the most terrifying part of it all was when he smiled.

He had the kind of smile the devil himself must have designed.

Her wolf whimpered and clawed at Luna's insides. She didn't want out. Didn't want to confront the man that had hurt them and the people they loved. She was too scared, too terrified for that. No, her wolf was clawing to get deeper, to hide. She wanted as far away from this man as possible and Luna didn't even blame her.

But she refused to cower.

Luna tilted her chin up to meet his cold eyes head on. She refused to show him her fear. He liked it too much. Fed on it. She'd learned that about him early on and she refused to feed this monster. She purposefully held herself still when he grabbed a stool and propped it in front of her, casually climbing atop it as if they were going to share a beer at a bar. She kept her face blank even if she had to knot her fingers together to stop her hands from shaking.

"Hello, my love." He smirked, "How are you feeling this evening?"

Luna narrowed her eyes but didn't respond. He didn't actually care how she was feeling. She knew that. If he did, he wouldn't have kept her chained up on a full moon, bound by silver and unable to turn. If he cared about her at all he wouldn't have murdered and kidnapped her family, held her here in the basement as some sort of toy to play with so long as she amused him.

He was up to something. She knew that much. He had a plan for her. She was nowhere close to giving in to it so she didn't understand the smile on his face, the one that said he'd won.

What had he done now?

"Are you feeling a little pained perhaps?" He tilted his head curiously, "Maybe feel like you've been gutted? They say mates can feel that sort of thing but I've always wondered if it happens even before a bond is forged. When he dies, do you think you'll feel that too?"

Luna fought a flinch of shock and horror. Her mate? Gutted? Dying? Was that why the pain tonight was so much worse? She'd thought it was the full moon. She bit her lip and refused to give anything away when he smirked as if he already knew the answer.

This. This was why she was so certain her brother was still alive. Because if he wasn't, if this homicidal, delusional, narcissistic psychopath had killed Leo he wouldn't have kept her in the dark about it. He would have been down here bragging. He'd have dragged Leo's lifeless, headless body down the steps and tossed it at her feet while he laughed. So yes, Leo was still alive.

And, from the foul mood permeating the air, so was her mate... whoever he was.

Luna didn't know who he was and she had no idea how this psycho had figured it out. He could be bluffing but... A sick feeling of dread curled through her veins and her wolf whimpered again. There was only one way he could know for sure, one way that he could be so smug about it.

Nova. Her youngest sister. She'd been having visions since she was four years old. She was a Seer. It was a gift, but also a curse. It meant she could see the future and sometimes that was a good thing but in Nova's case, it almost always came with a glimpse of danger.

Her sweet, special sister who had accidentally set all of this in motion. Nova had seen a vision of Luna's future and she'd told them all about it. She'd said that Luna was destined to mate with an Alpha, but not in the Crescent pack. She'd said Luna would leave the pack when her mate came for her and that she would rule over a new pack, giving them a strong alliance.

The news had been... unbelievable to say the least. Because Luna wasn't a dominant wolf. She was submissive and every shifter worth their weight knew that an Alpha needed a strong female at his side. If the Alpha female weren't strong she'd be challenged by the more dominant wolves in the pack relentlessly. Luna had never worried about it, had never even given it a thought. She'd dismissed Nova's claims as the silly dreams of a child that wanted her big sister to find her happily ever after.

But it hadn't mattered that Luna didn't believe... because Maddox had.

Maddox Clary, who was cruel and sadistic and took pleasure in causing others pain. Maddox who had always thought *he* should have been born to rule the pack, not Leo. Maddox who was so desperate for power that there were rumors he'd killed his own littermate simply so he would be the sole heir in his family. Maddox who had set his sights on her from the moment he walked into Crescent territory for reasons she'd never understood. Not until it was too late.

He didn't want her. Not really. He wanted what she represented. He wanted what she would offer a mate. Her standing in the pack. Her connections and royal blood. And he'd liked the idea of having a submissive wolf at his side, someone that wouldn't challenge him or put up too much of a fight.

That was where he'd made his mistake.

He'd thought because her wolf was submissive that she would accept his claim. He'd thought he could force her into marrying him. He'd murdered her father, at the very least run her brother off, and he'd intended to claim her and take control of the Crescent pack but he'd misjudged her.

Her wolf was submissive. She wasn't. And she would never agree to take a claim that wasn't from her true mate. Let alone from someone that had ripped her family apart.

Her father was dead. He'd told her that her mother died of a broken heart not long after. It was the way of the bond.

Very few mates were strong enough to survive if their other half was taken from them suddenly and violently.

Her parents were dead. Her siblings had been ripped away from her. She knew he had Nova and Maya hidden somewhere nearby, held as captives. And Leo... God, where was her brother?

Not dead. She was sure of it now. But where then? And why hadn't he come for them yet? She had no idea. If anyone could know where he was it was...

A sickening thought hit her and she snapped her eyes back to his, "You're using Nova for her visions. What have you done to her? What did you threaten to make her tell you anything?"

"Always with the accusations." Maddox chirped disapprovingly.

"What'd you do to my sister?"

"Nothing." His eyes flashed in the dark light, "Yet. And so long as she keeps telling me about the visions she has, then nothing will happen to her. You have my word."

Luna swallowed roughly past her wolf who was clawing at her throat, "She's had more visions?"

"Mhmm."

"And you made her tell you about them." She felt sick again at the thought that her sister might have given away Leo's location, wherever it may be.

"I don't make the Seer do anything." He tsked, "But she's a smart girl. Smarter than you. See, she knows what it would mean for her sisters if she lied to me or tried to keep me in the dark. She knows I'll hurt someone she loves if she doesn't do what I ask."

"Ask." Luna spit the word at him, "You mean order."

"I'm an Alpha. It's what I was made for." He snarled right back, "Just like you were made to submit to me. And you will, Luna. You will or I will do more than just threaten your sisters."

Bile rose in her throat at the thought. She was getting accustomed to the threats though. He always threatened her when he came down here but as far as she knew, he'd never followed through and hurt her sisters. He didn't want her to hate him. He wanted her to choose him. Love him even. Or, more likely, worship him. He wanted her at his side to unite the pack that was still splintered after what he'd done to her father. He wanted her and he wouldn't lose her easily.

Something he'd said finally clicked into place in her foggy, malnourished head and she squinted in the darkness, "Nova saw who my true mate is, didn't she? She saw him and she knew he was coming for me. Just like she said he would."

In the original vision, Nova hadn't known the identity of Luna's mate. She hadn't been able to see him. She'd just known that he was an Alpha and that he was from another pack. But Maddox had said he attacked him tonight, which meant...

"Something changed." She gasped, "Fate changed and she saw him more clearly didn't she? She was right? He's an Alpha?"

Maddox snarled, "It doesn't matter what he is. He can't come for you now. I made sure of that. All he's going to have time for is to heal for the next few days and by then, you're going to agree to be mine."

"He's... not dead then?" A small hope that she'd never let bloom inside her before sprouted. There was someone out there that could come for her after all. Her mate. Whoever he was. "You didn't kill him?"

"Not for lack of trying." Maddox growled, "Your bitch sister forgot to mention that the True Alpha was back and that feral bastard caught me off guard. He got between us and we had to retreat. But we did enough damage to keep them at bay for a while."

Luna's head spun, "True Alpha?"

"Don't give yourself a headache, love. That fucked up family isn't your concern. It's mine. I already spoke to the Seer again. She says your mate will heal and he'll come for you in three days time." He met her eyes seriously, "So that's how long I'm giving you to make the right decision and accept my offer."

Hope. That tiny, morsel of hope died a cruel and unusual death. He snuffed it out as quickly as it had sprouted.

Three days. She only had three days. Three more days and then...

"If you don't change your mind and accept my claim on you, I'll kill Maya. She's of no use to me. I had thought I'd simply wait for her to come of age and claim her instead but she's too dominant, too headstrong. You're the one I want. Agree to be my queen and I'll let her live. More than that, I'll make sure your true mate dies quickly. Don't and I'll torture them both in front of you until you go mad and then I'll just wait for Nova to come of age to claim her instead."

Luna shuddered at the threat. He wasn't offering her anything. Not really. He wasn't offering to let her mate live. He'd only said he would kill him quickly. But he wasn't Luna's concern. Not really. She could live without her mate if she had to but she couldn't live with knowing she was the reason her sister was tortured and murdered right along with their parents.

A tear slipped down her cheek and she made no move to wipe it away. Maddox smirked. That smug smile of his made sense now. He knew she was out of time. He knew when her mate would come for her and he'd kill him. But worse than that, he knew she would never leave her sisters to his cruelty. Either Maya died and Nova was forced into a claim with this psycho or Luna took it on herself and kept her sisters safe.

Was there even a choice left?

"Oh, and just to sweeten the pot. I'll tell you who your mate is if you want. Wouldn't want you saying I didn't give you all the information to make an informed decision."

Pain made her eyes meet his. The only reason he'd offer to tell her who her mate was now was to hurt her. He wanted to torture her some more.

"I don't want to know." She blurted out.

He smirked, "Too bad."

Maddox pushed himself up off the stool and put it aside like he always did when he was readying to leave. But he moved a little slower than he normally did, she noticed. Was he hurt? He'd obviously fought her mate tonight and he hadn't walked away as unscathed as he wanted her to believe.

"Michael Hudson, Alpha of the Moirae pack even though he was last in line for it. Strong wolf. Smart wolf. I'd commend him on knocking his brothers out of their rightful inheritance but I won't get that chance. He'll be dead soon so it doesn't really matter."

Luna whimpered as her wolf clawed at her again. Her wolf howled and cried out at the thought of losing her mate, even if she hadn't met him yet. She knew the name. She knew he was a good man. He was a good Alpha. But he couldn't save her.

She would never meet him. Never get to know him. Never mate and make pups and have a family with him. He would die and he would be just another name she had to add to her list because it would be all her fault.

Her cheeks were wet and her eyes were blurry when she glanced back up at the monster in front of her. She was crying, she realized. Crying for all of the things she'd lost. All she still had left to lose. But not this. She wouldn't let anyone else die for her. Michael Hudson, her mate, couldn't save her but just maybe she could save him.

"Okay." She sniffled.

Maddox paused, "What?"

Confusion flashed in his gaze, as if he hadn't truly expected her to speak. He'd thought she would cower and cry until the last minute. But he'd known what her answer would be and when the confusion turned smug and knowing she broke and stared at her bound wrists and ankles instead.

"Okay." She forced the words that would mean her own doom out, "I'll accept your claim if you swear not to kill anyone else."

A slow, evil smile spread across his handsome face and Luna fell into the pit of despair that had been trying to swallow her whole for weeks.

"Deal."

To Be Continued...

COMING SOON

Unbelievable Faith
Book 2 in the Fated Mates Duet

Fate can be cruel.

Luna DeLuca has lost everything except for her faith in herself. Kidnapped, tortured and threatened by a male that's already killed half her family, she knows the only way to save the other half is by offering herself up to him. To save her sisters, she's willing to do anything, even accept a claim from a male that isn't her mate, a mark on her soul that will ruin her forever. But if this is what her family needs, what her pack needs, she'll do it to save them all.

Fate can be twisted.

Michael Hudson thought his mission to save the neighboring Crescent pack was about helping out a friend. He thought it was about avenging an attack on his own. But the second he sets his eyes on the beautiful girl locked away in a dank basement he knows she's why he was put on the face of this planet. She's the reason he's here. She's everything. She's his. His mate. His fate. His future. Only, she bears the scent of another and is nothing like what he imagined his fated mate to be.

But fate can also be kind.

As brave as she is, Luna's wolf is submissive and submissive wolves aren't meant to lead packs. They aren't meant to be Queens. She knows that. So does Michael. But when he refuses to give up on her, refuses to walk away or back down, she begins to see why fate put them together. She softens him and he strengthens her and maybe, just maybe, if they believe in fate enough they can find their way to forever.

ACKNOWLEDGMENTS

Every time I go to write this part of a book, I get a little emotional.

You know what they say about it taking a village to raise a child? Well, the same goes for a book baby. Nobody writes and publishes a novel alone even if it's self-published. It's a journey and the person that kept me going when I doubted myself most was you, the reader.

Thank you for all of your messages, likes, comments and support. You make all of this worthwhile. Thanks for sticking with me as I branch into yet another new genre. I hope you enjoyed this little detour into the paranormal world of shifter romance as much as I did. Sometimes we all just need a break from reality, right?

Lesley – I don't know how I managed this thing called life without you. You make me laugh when I'm feeling down. You keep me sane when I spiral. You're always there to remind me that I am neither the first nor the last person to believe it when people call me crazy (and to tell me that crazy isn't necessarily a bad thing). Thank you for always believing in me.

Maren – How could I have known doing a silly bookstagram challenge would lead me to my other half. Thank you for listening to me bitch and whine. Thank you for reminding me that this is supposed to be fun. Thank you for your support day in and day out. It means the world to me.

Laura – Your wisdom and guidance are immeasurable. You're like a fairy godmother sprinkling us all in your brilliance. Too much? In short, you're amazing and I'm lucky to call you friend.

Xoxo, Jess

ABOUT THE AUTHOR

Jess Bryant is an avid indoorswoman. A city girl trapped in a country girl's life, her heart resides in Dallas but her soul and roots are in small town Oklahoma. She enjoys manicures, the color pink, and her completely impractical for country life stilettos. She believes that hair color is a legitimate form of therapy, as is reading and writing romance. She started writing as a little girl but her life changed forever when she stole a book from her aunt's Harlequin collection and she's been creating love stories with happily ever afters ever since.

Jess holds a degree in Public Relations from the University of Oklahoma and is a lifetime supporter of her school and athletic teams. And why not? They have a ton of National Championships! She may be a girlie girl but she knows her sports stats and isn't afraid to tell you that your school isn't as cool as hers... or that your sports romance got it all wrong.

For more information on Jess and upcoming releases, contact her at jessbryantbooks@gmail.com or follow her on her many social media accounts for news and shenanigans.

ALSO AVAILABLE FROM JESS BRYANT

The West Brothers Series

Crazy Little Thing Called Love

Something To Talk About

Too Good To Be True

Merry Little Christmas (A West Brothers Novella)

Stand-Alone

It Had To Be You

Call Me, Irresistible

Stay A Little Longer (A M/M Novella)

Bomar Boys Series

No Regrets

No Apologies

No Fear

Nothing to Lose (Coming Soon)

Anthologies & Co-Writes

Rounding Third: A Baseball Anthology

CALL ME, IRRESISTIBLE

A Fate, Texas Novel

Impulsive. Irresponsible. Impossible.

Lemon Kelly lives in a world that is fast, loud and a little bit crazy. She left her small hometown for the bright lights of Nashville and has been living her dream ever since. She's traveled the world and plays her music for crowds of adoring fans. She has everything she ever wanted. Only the wants of a 17 year old girl vary greatly from the needs of a grown woman. Is it selfish to want something more, something like the love she writes songs about?

Can a girl have two dreams? Or will she have to give up one to get the other? And if so... which? Fame or a family of her own?

Stable. Solid. Safe.

Shane Lowry likes his quiet, controlled life. The always responsible small town deputy is a father to his three daughters first and foremost. Nothing comes before them. He had to grow up fast and early and he's long since stopped letting silly things like lust control his actions. He doesn't even date. So why does he find himself so drawn to the lively girl next door turned country music superstar that is the complete opposite of what he should want in a woman?

If he lets her in, she'll shake up his entire world. He knows it. But is that a good thing or a very bad thing?

The sparks between them are undeniable. The pull irresistible. And if they take a chance they just might find what they've both been missing.

Call Me, Irresistible is a standalone, full length, contemporary romance novel set in Fate, Texas with a guaranteed HEA. It is intended for audiences 18+ due to language and sexual situations. If you enjoy the quirky characters in this little town, try other releases by Jess Bryant set in Fate such as the West Brothers Series.

IT HAD TO BE YOU

A Fate, Texas Novel

Austin Evans is a playboy, a flirt and a charmer. He's dated half the female population of Fate, Texas and figures he'll get around to the other half before he ever decides to settle down. Fate, however, has other ideas. Because one night with the prim and proper town doctor isn't nearly enough. He can't get her out of his head, doesn't want her out of his bed and if he can convince her to give him half a chance he'll keep her in his life forever.

It was supposed to be one night. One night of passion. One night of scorching hot, mind-blowing, earth-rocking fun. It was a one night stand that somehow turned into two nights, then three and four... and Victoria Sands knew better. Of course she knew better. She was a good girl, a smart girl. She knew better than to continue seeking him out, knew better than to keep falling into his arms, knew better than to let her heart get involved, but when it came to Austin her logical, rational brain never stood a chance to her body's desire.

They're complete opposites. She's the town princess and he's the boy from the wrong side of the tracks. She grew up in the mansion on the hill and his mother is the woman that cleans it. She thinks everything through and he goes with his gut instinct. The one thing they have in common is that they've never felt anything like the sparks that flare between them.

But is that enough to build a life on? A family on? And what about forever?

27992125R00144

Made in the USA
Lexington, KY
09 January 2019